Samuel French Acting Edition

Thespian Playworks 2017

Flopsie
by Nick Krentel

Pigeon!
by Garrett M. Ryan

Talking to Your Child About Death
by Bella Yaguda

Waylen
by Kayla Temshiv

SAMUELFRENCH.COM   SAMUELFRENCH.CO.UK

FOR PRODUCTION ENQUIRIES

UNITED STATES AND CANADA
Info@SamuelFrench.com
1-866-598-8449

UNITED KINGDOM AND EUROPE
Plays@SamuelFrench.co.uk
020-7255-4302

Each title is subject to availability from Samuel French, depending upon country of performance. Please be aware that THESPIAN PLAYWORKS 2017 may not be licensed by Samuel French in your territory. Professional and amateur producers should contact the nearest Samuel French office or licensing partner to verify availability.

MUSIC USE NOTE

Licensees are solely responsible for obtaining formal written permission from copyright owners to use copyrighted music in the performance of this play and are strongly cautioned to do so. If no such permission is obtained by the licensee, then the licensee must use only original music that the licensee owns and controls. Licensees are solely responsible and liable for all music clearances and shall indemnify the copyright owners of the play(s) and their licensing agent, Samuel French, against any costs, expenses, losses and liabilities arising from the use of music by licensees. Please contact the appropriate music licensing authority in your territory for the rights to any incidental music.

IMPORTANT BILLING AND CREDIT REQUIREMENTS

If you have obtained performance rights to this title, please refer to your licensing agreement for important billing and credit requirements.

ABOUT THESPIAN PLAYWORKS

Thespian Playworks is a writing contest and script-development program for high school students, sponsored by the Educational Theatre Association and run by the staff of *Dramatics* magazine. Each year, up to four finalists are invited to the International Thespian Festival, where the students work with a professional director, a dramaturg, and a volunteer cast of actors to put their short plays on their feet before a live audience.

Launched in 1994 as a tribute to longtime International Thespian Society executive Doug Finney, the program aims to nurture young playwrights, and over Playworks' history, many participants have gone on to college majors and careers in theatre, writing, and related fields. Whatever the eventual future of the writers or their scripts, Playworks is an exhilarating experience in a creative discipline seldom taught in schools or celebrated in the wider culture.

The call for entries goes out each fall, with submission deadlines in mid-winter. *Dramatics* receives scores of scripts from high school thespians all over the U.S., Canada, and as far away as the United Arab Emirates. Each play is reviewed at least twice, as teams of readers (including *Dramatics* staff and other professional critics and theatre artists) narrow down the entries: first to a dozen semifinalists, then to the final four. Each semifinalist receives a personal letter with feedback on his or her script.

For more on Thespian Playworks, please visit www.edta.org/playworks.

CONTENTS

Flopsie 7

Pigeon! 39

Talking to Your Child About Death 71

Waylen 87

FLOPSIE

Nick Krentel

FLOPSIE, by Nick Krentel of Troupe 7014 at Seven Lakes High School in Katy, Texas, was presented in a staged reading as part of the Thespian Playworks program at the 2017 International Thespian Festival on June 24, 2017. The production was directed by Bill Myatt, with dramaturgy by Stephen Gregg, and assistant direction by Emma Oppenheimer. The stage manager was Jessica Gable. The cast was as follows:

MARY . . . . Maris Turner
SUSAN . . . . Katie Markle
GEORGE . . . . Parker Koch
JANIS . . . . Amrutha Santashkumar
FLOPSIE / MAX . . . . Josh Gelman
FLOPSIE / JOHN . . . . Jared Bowen-Kauth
FLOPSIE / CLAIRE . . . . Emma Smith

CHARACTERS

MARY
SUSAN – her mother
GEORGE – her father
JANIS – her neighbor
FLOPSIE – a dragon
MAX
JOHN – his father
CLAIRE – his mother

SETTING

The set is an enormous bedroom with a large, arching window and various moving boxes compiled in it. The room is so large that it has its own miniature living room down center with two plush yet elegant armchairs, a matching couch, and a coffee table in between them. The bed is located upstage left with an accompanying nightstand and lamp. There is also a large double door leading to the closet upstage right with black scorch marks surrounding it. The room should feel slightly empty – even though it is fully decorated – because of just how expansive it really is.

Scene One: Moving Day

(**SUSAN** *and* **GEORGE** *enter, out of breath, carrying gigantic boxes.* **MARY** *enters carrying three bankers boxes stacked so high that you can barely see her when she's facing straight-on.*)

SUSAN. Oh, Sugar, you've hardly broken a sweat! What's in those boxes, blankets?

MARY. Books and dictionaries.

SUSAN. I thought we were carrying the books. What did we bring up then?

(**GEORGE** *opens one of the boxes he brought up.*)

GEORGE. Feather pillows.

SUSAN. Huh.

(*Beat.*)

Well, Mary, look at your new room! Isn't it gorgeous? Look at how big it is.

(*Looking around.*)

I honestly think this is bigger than the entire first floor of our old house.

GEORGE. And we got this house for a steal too! It's amazing how the mysterious disappearances of all the previous owners can really lower the property value of an old-school mansion like this one.

SUSAN. But we still had to dip into your college account to afford it!

(*The adults laugh.*)

GEORGE. And we're not even kidding, Sparkles, there is no way you can go to college unless you earn several scholarships!

(*They both laugh again.*)

SUSAN & GEORGE. Ahhhh, finances.

(*Beat.*)

SUSAN. So do you like your new room, Mary?

MARY. I guess...

GEORGE. I guess? Why so glum chum? Sadness leads to madness. Look at how big this is!

(*He runs around and does some sort of aerobic activity like sprinting laps, dancing ballet, cartwheels, backflips, etc. Anything works.*)

LOOK AT ALL OF THE FUN THINGS YOU CAN DO IN HERE!

MARY. Yeah, I guess the extra room is nice...but the scorch marks are a little disconcerting.

GEORGE. Ooooo, great vocabulary there missy. Colleges love some good SAT words! Besides, I thought it was just a funky fresh paint preference for the previous patrons of this happy home.

SUSAN. Yes, I think I read that scorch marks were all the rage in Paris right now.

(*Beat.*)

Or was that colorful socks?

MARY. (*Under her breath.*) Definitely socks.

GEORGE. What was that, Kitten?

MARY. Nothing.

GEORGE. (*Very slightly unhinged.*) No, it wasn't. You said *something*, not *nothing*. And by saying that you said nothing you are in the proximity of *lying*! And I-I-I-

(**GEORGE** *takes a deep breath and regains composure.*)

SUSAN. You know how your father feels about lying, Mary.

ALL. Lying is the equivalent of dying, and a good family never lies. We are a good family; we never lie.

> *(Enter **JANIS** carrying a mouthwatering cherry pie with a lattice crust.)*

JANIS. *(Chipper and bright.)* Knock, knock! Special delivery! I heard yelling, so I just decided to follow the voices.

GEORGE. Oh, hello there, come on in! That was me you heard. I AM GEORGE HARDING AND THIS IS MY WIFE SUSAN AND OUR DAUGHTER, MARY!

JANIS. *(Unfazed.)* Pleasure to meet you both Mr. and Mrs. Harding. I'm Janis Bourland. I live right next door, and, seeing as it's the neighborly thing to do, I brought over a fresh pie to welcome you to Mountain Lake Terrace: Colorado's finest and most exclusive neighborhood!

SUSAN. *(Taking the pie.)* Why, thank you. That's very sweet.

GEORGE. Let's hope the pie is too!

> *(**JANIS** bursts into over-exaggerated, fake laughter: the trademark of an obvious kiss-ass.)*

JANIS. Oh, my! Mrs. Harding, you have bagged yourself quite the comedian.

SUSAN. That I have. George, let's go find the plates and utensils. I'm sure the two of you would like to talk alone for a little bit.

MARY. Um, hi. Sorry about my dad, he gets excited easily –

> *(**JANIS** envelops **MARY** into the biggest of hugs.)*

JANIS. Oh, my god! It is so nice to meet you. I just know we're gonna be the best of friends!

SUSAN & GEORGE. Awwww!

> *(Smiling, they exit the room.)*

MARY. You know, I was a little scared I was gonna be alone here, but –

JANIS. Let me stop you right there. You and I, we are not friends. What I gave your parents is a welcome of neighborly sorts; what I'm giving to you here is a welcome to reality. You're a nobody, and that piece of junk Camry just screams "I'm a part of the middle class!" so I'm guessing you moved here for the school district and booming job market, but only got the house because the previous owners were murdered or something.

MARY. Wait, murdered?

JANIS. Or something. Oh, my god, they had the most annoying six-year-old son. All he could talk about was trains. Do those even exist anymore?

MARY. Well, Amtrak –

JANIS. It was a rhetorical question. I'm not an idiot. Let's get back to the point, shall we? Don't answer that. Look, I've been at the bottom of the social ladder, and I'm not going back. If it had been a couple of years ago, like before I got my nose job or something, I'm sure you and I would have been the best of buds. But that's not gonna happen here. And when school starts in a couple of months, don't you dare talk to me. Actually, don't even look at me. I've got a reputation to uphold, and I don't need your lousy, new girl neediness rubbing off on me. Got it?

MARY. I –

JANIS. *(Exiting.)* Great. I'm gonna bail; there is no way in hell I'm eating a slice of that lard bomb when your whacko parents return.

> (**MARY** *is alone. She walks around the room, taking it in. She takes a deep breath. She walks over to a box on top of her bed and begins to unpack it. It contains sweaters, a stuffed giraffe, a rubber-band ball, some miscellaneous knickknacks and trinkets like ribbons and snow globes, and, finally, a picture in a frame. None of these faze her,*

until she reaches the picture. She lifts it out of the box very slowly and sits on her bed. She mournfully stares at the picture for a long time. She begins to cry. Not a loud bawl, but the sort of soft cry that only happens when you just can't keep your sadness locked inside any longer. She wipes her tears and swallows her sadness. She then places the picture on the nightstand and the audience can finally see it. It's a picture of Mary and her friends. She turns off the lights and crawls into bed. She begins to very softly cry again.)

(Blackout.)

Scene Two: The First Night

(It's dark. Moonlight pours in through the window. MARY is gently sleeping in her bed, clutching her giraffe. The closet doors open slowly. The sound of large claws scraping the floorboards is heard as certain boxes begin to move, as if being pushed out of the way by some invisible force. The force hits a box with a snow globe on top of it, and the snow globe falls and shatters. MARY jolts awake.)

MARY. Hello? Mom, Dad, is that you?

(She squints in the dark, looking around.)

Hello, is anybody there?

(As she reaches toward the lamp on her nightstand, the giant window begins to open. Having trouble finding the lamp's switch:)

Dad, if this is some kind of joke, it's not very funny.

(The windows fly open and a loud flapping noise is heard. MARY screams. Her parents burst through the door in matching his and hers pajamas.)

GEORGE. Sweetheart, are you alright? We heard you scream.

MARY. How did you get here so fast?

GEORGE. Nothing is faster than a concerned parent, my child.

SUSAN. Plus, we had fallen asleep at your door after drinking the glass of warm milk we were originally going to bring to you.

MARY. Quick, check the room, there's someone in here!

(The parents search the room. They check under her bed...nothing. They look in boxes, both big and small...nothing. They look under the coffee table at the same time and scare themselves. Then they check the closet.)

> **GEORGE** *begins to open the doors very slowly.*
> *He then jerks them open and a box falls on top*
> *of him. He shrieks like a child. The screams of*
> *terror continue until –)*

SUSAN. George, calm down, it was just a box!

GEORGE. *(Instantly calm.)* Oh, really? How silly of me.

> *(They both share an over-exaggerated laugh.)*

MARY. *(Timid.)* Are they gone?

SUSAN. Are you sure there was someone here?

MARY. Yes, I heard them!

GEORGE. But did you see them?

MARY. No, but I heard something break.

SUSAN. That was your snow globe. I saw it smashed on the floor.

MARY. *(Getting defensive.)* See!

GEORGE. *(Jolly.)* It probably just fell over.

MARY. Then explain how the window opened.

GEORGE. The wind.

MARY. It opens outward.

GEORGE. Then it was the inside wind.

> *(**MARY** continues to get angrier and angrier*
> *at her father's dismissals. Meanwhile, he*
> *miraculously seems to get only more and*
> *more cheerful.)*

MARY. That's not a thing.

GEORGE. Yes, it is.

MARY. No, it's not!

GEORGE. Oh, my little golden nugget, I assure you it is!

MARY. What about the flapping noise I heard? I heard something that sounded like giant, flapping wings!

GEORGE. A bat.

MARY. A bat?!

GEORGE. Yes, a bat. This is an old house with tall ceilings. I bet what you heard was a bat flying around!

MARY. Are you an idiot?

SUSAN. Mary!

GEORGE. Wow, Pumpkin, that's a silly thing to say. Especially to your *father* who provided you with this lovely new home.

MARY. *(Sarcastic.) Yes*, a lovely new home that's infested with bats.

GEORGE. Exactly! I'm so glad you understand my delicious, cinnamon-dusted waffle!

> (**SUSAN** *picks up that* **GEORGE** *isn't reading the situation.)*

SUSAN. George, I think it's time we go back to bed.

GEORGE. If you say so, dear.

> *(They begin to exit.)*

Our sugarplum sure is acting funny isn't she?

SUSAN. She's just having trouble adjusting. You know kids and their overactive imaginations.

> *(They're gone.* **MARY** *is once again all alone. She gets up from bed and goes to shut the window. She looks up at the ceiling and then at the scorched closet.)*

MARY. It was just a bat, Mary. Just a bat.

> *(Blackout.)*

Scene Three: Family Picture Time

(A camera tripod is set up in Mary's room, facing the window. **GEORGE** *is messing with the camera, trying to make everything perfect for the picture.* **SUSAN** *and* **MARY** *sit on the couch together.)*

MARY. Tell me again why we are taking a family picture in my room.

SUSAN. He says that it has the best view of the topiary garden.

MARY. Right.

> *(**MARY** sighs.)*

SUSAN. Mary, are you okay?

MARY. It's just...I miss my friends. And Dad won't let me get a cell phone because he thinks that stupid Stephen King novel about cell phones turning people into zombies is a warning from Stephen *Haw*-king. He does know they're two different people, right?

> *(**SUSAN** laughs.)*

SUSAN. I'm sure he does, Sweetheart.

MARY. Please don't call me Sweetheart.

SUSAN. Why not?

MARY. It sounds like something *he* would say.

SUSAN. What do you mean?

MARY. He never calls me Mary; it's always Sweetheart, or Sparkles, or Honeybear, or some other nickname.

SUSAN. That's just because he loves you very much.

MARY. Does he really though?

> *(The camera's flash goes off while* **GEORGE** *is standing right in front of it. He falls down in surprise.)*

SUSAN. *(In a whisper.)* Mary! How could you say such a thing? Of course your father loves you!

MARY. I don't know... It's just that he acts so weird, and when you're with him *you* act so weird too. I mean when it's just you and me you act like a normal mother, but when he's around it's like we're on planet weirdo!

SUSAN. There is no such thing as a normal mother, Mary. But yes, I will admit your father does have an effect on me. Growing up, I lived a very "normal" life: nothing out of the ordinary, just me and my parents. They loved each other, not passionately, but still loved each other nonetheless. They were both always busy with their individual work, so the house was usually quiet. No other siblings to give the house character or noise. Just pure, quiet nothingness for me to do my school work until my parents returned from work. And even then they never said much. It wasn't until I met your father in college that my life became any form of the word "exciting." He was so full of energy – he still is mind you. And his smile radiated heat that would rival a microwave oven. He was handsome, and kind, and all-around just a warm ray of light in my life. His happiness seeped into my own and I adopted his smile. I started to act like him and say all of those stupid phrases he says like "a smile goes a mile" and "kindness leads to mindness."

> *(She says with a chuckle:)*

I mean, what does that even mean? But I digress; your father is like a disease, and I got a full-blown infection. I couldn't help it – and neither could he. He didn't have the stable life that I grew up with. His was nothing but chaos. His father left when he was very young, and his mother struggled to take care of him and his two brothers. His life was never simple, but, still, he acquired this persona of idiotic bliss, and I fell madly in love with him for it. I know your father's not perfect, but he could be a lot worse...and he does love you very much. As do I.

GEORGE. I think the camera is ready!

SUSAN. Okay, honey, we'll be there in a second.

(*Aside to* **MARY**.) I know this is hard, Mary, but your father wanted to give you what he never had: a lovely home and a perfect family.

MARY. But I'm not perfect, and I don't think I can be.

SUSAN. Yes you are, just being yourself is perfect enough for the whole world.

MARY. Thank you, Mom. I really do appreciate it.

SUSAN. Anytime, my sweet Mary. Do you think you can muster up a smile for a few pictures?

MARY. I'll try my hardest.

GEORGE. Are you guys coming?

SUSAN. Right this second. Come on Mary, let's go.

(*She takes her hand and they walk to the camera.* **SUSAN** *and* **GEORGE** *stand in the back with* **MARY** *up front between them. They reflect the perfect, happy family. The camera flashes.*)

(*Blackout.*)

Scene Four: Enter The Beast

> (*It's night.* **MARY** *is sleeping. She looks peaceful. Some time has passed. The room is now decorated more to Mary's, or possibly her father's, taste. It's quiet. Suddenly, the closet door creaks open.* **MARY** *jolts awake, holding a baseball bat.*)

MARY. I warn you, I'm armed!

> (*The closet shuts immediately.* **MARY** *gets out of bed and creeps slowly toward the closet.*)

Also, my dad is trained in judo, taekwondo, and Brazilian jiu-jitsu... And my mom has a shotgun.

> (*She's at the closet. Her hand trembles as she reaches toward the knob.*)

You can do this, Mary.

> (*She yanks the door open.* **MARY** *drops the bat in shock. It's a dragon...but the audience can't see this.* **MARY** *falls backward onto her hands.*)

Oh, my god.

> (*The dragon begins to speak. It is the voice of a young boy. His voice is projected from a microphone backstage.*)

FLOPSIE. Wait! Please don't be scared! Hi, I'm Flophavin-gava-kanafkin, but you can call me Flopsie for short.

MARY. You're...a...dragon.

FLOPSIE. Yep, that's correct.

MARY. Named Flop–Flopha–ha–ha–havin–

FLOPSIE. Flopsie.

MARY. Named Flopsie.

> (*Beat.*)

Okay, so this is definitely a dream.

FLOPSIE. This is not a dream.

MARY. This is not a dream? How do I know this is not a dream?

FLOPSIE. It's just...not. Does it feel like you're dreaming?

MARY. No.

FLOPSIE. Then you're not.

MARY. Okay, so I'm not dreaming... That only means I've lost my mind and gone insane.

FLOPSIE. *(Laughing.)* You're not insane! I'm real!

MARY. How am I supposed to know if you're real?!

FLOPSIE. Touch me.

MARY. What?

FLOPSIE. Go on, touch me. When you imagine...I don't know...a bed, yeah, when you imagine a bed and try to jump on you just fall through. So, if your mind is making me up, then your hand will just fall through, but if I'm real, you'll feel something back. Make sense?

MARY. I guess?

FLOPSIE. Then come on, lay a hand on me. I won't bite, I promise.

MARY. You swear?

FLOPSIE. With all my dragon honor.

MARY. Is that a thing?

FLOPSIE. No, but it sounds cool, doesn't it?

> (**MARY** *giggles and smiles a real, warm, genuine smile.*)

You have a really beautiful smile.

MARY. Oh, thank you. I...I think I'm going to touch you now.

FLOPSIE. Okay. Take your time.

> (**MARY** *slowly walks toward* **FLOPSIE**, *analyzing his every detail. She takes a big breath, extends her arm, and, very gently, touches* **FLOPSIE***'s side.*)

MARY. You're – you're cold. And you're...real. What are you doing in my room?

FLOPSIE. Well, I actually live here...in your closet. It's surprisingly roomy! But that's beside the point. I – um – well – I've been hearing you cry.

MARY. Oh.

FLOPSIE. And I just wanted to tell you that you don't have to be alone.

MARY. I don't?

FLOPSIE. I'd like to be your...friend. If you're interested, of course. I'm sort of alone too. My parents left me a while back.

MARY. I'm...so sorry.

FLOPSIE. It's fine, really. We were never that close. They never really "got me." You know what I mean?

MARY. Yeah, I do.

(**MARY** *sighs.*)

FLOPSIE. Oh god, I'm being depressing. I'm not normally like this; in fact, I'm usually a ton of fun. Being a dragon has its perks, you know. I mean there's the flying, the super strength, and the huge tail. It has a ton of uses: like, if you wanted to, we could use it as a jump rope or something!

(**FLOPSIE** *gives a demonstration. There is a loud "swoosh" as he swings his tail. His tail collides with one of the chairs downstage, causing it to fly off the ground and shatter.*)

Oops.

MARY. *(Laughing.)* I'm gonna go with "or something" for the tail.

FLOPSIE. Yeah, you're right.

MARY. My dad is so going to ground me.

FLOPSIE. Sorry, adults are so stupid. On the bright side, it means we can get to know each other better. Speaking of adults, your parents can't see me.

MARY. What?

FLOPSIE. I'm invisible to whoever I choose. I wanted you to see me, and now you can, but, for the most part, dragons stay in hiding to keep safe from being hunted and such.

MARY. Okay.

FLOPSIE. Yeah, I know it's a lot to take in, but I'd really like to be your friend. Being alone sucks.

MARY. Yeah, it does

>*(Beat.)*

Okay.

FLOPSIE. Okay?

MARY. Okay, let's do it; let's be friends!

FLOPSIE. Really?

MARY. Yeah, really.

>*(**MARY** reaches out to shake **FLOPSIE**'s paw/ talons.)*

Hi, Flopsie. I'm Mary Harding, and it's a pleasure to be your friend!

FLOPSIE. You have no idea how happy you've made me!

>*(They shake on it.)*

MARY. Wow, your skin really is ice-cold. That's not at all what I expected.

FLOPSIE. What did you expect?

MARY. I don't know...warmth I guess. Dragons breathe fire, so –

FLOPSIE. Dragons don't breathe fire.

MARY. Dragons don't breathe fire?

FLOPSIE. No, we don't. We eat fire.

MARY. You eat fire.

FLOPSIE. We eat fire and other flammable stuff.

MARY. Like what?

FLOPSIE. Let's see, fireworks, gasoline, petroleum, uranium, and liquid magma... And really spicy Indian food.

MARY. Well, we don't have any uranium, but we've got some tabasco sauce if you're hungry?

FLOPSIE. Not right now, but thanks for the offer.

MARY. Anytime.

FLOPSIE. Is there anything else about dragons you'd like to know?

MARY. I guess...everything.

FLOPSIE. Awesome.

(Lights begin to slowly fade to black.)

Well, it all begins in the snowy fjords of Sweden, the home of the dragons...

(Blackout.)

Scene Five: Talking To The Air

(**GEORGE** *is sitting on the couch reading a newspaper titled "New News for New News Readers."* **SUSAN** *is next to him knitting a scarf, and* **MARY** *is off near the closet talking to* **FLOPSIE.** **SUSAN** *has stopped knitting. She is watching* **MARY,** *very concerned.*)

GEORGE. Honey, listen to this, I'm reading this article on corn and...it...is...deee-lightful! Apparently corn is an almost perfect source of energy and ninety-five percent of all corn produced is field corn, but, get this, field corn is different from sweet corn, which is what canned corn and corn on the cob is. Mind...equals...blown. Also, field corn is used in alcohol and corn chips and ethanol and like all the corn preservatives. It's everywhere... we cannot escape it. If field corn became sentient and decided to wipe out the entire human race, it would definitely succeed...so let's pray that never happens!

(*Beat.*)

Also, in England, the word for corn is maize. A-maize-ing!

SUSAN. That's...that's nice, George.

GEORGE. You stopped knitting.

SUSAN. What?

GEORGE. Knitting. You stopped. Is something wrong?

SUSAN. Oh...it's nothing. I'm just worried about Mary.

GEORGE. Why? Our little pumpernickel looks like she's finally bucked up! See that smile? It's almost as beautiful as yours.

(*He leans over and starts kissing her neck.*)

SUSAN. (*Laughing.*) George, stop. Mary's right over there.

GEORGE. She's not looking; she's busy playing with her imaginary friend.

SUSAN. That's exactly what I'm worried about. Don't you think she's a little old to be talking to an imaginary friend?

GEORGE. Not at all! I had a pet rock named Farmsworth that I was friends with all throughout high school.

SUSAN. Wait, I thought Farmsworth was the guy who stole your first girlfriend?

GEORGE. That's why we stopped talking. Ol' Farmy had a way with the ladies and I could never compete.

SUSAN. George, I'm being serious!

GEORGE. Fine! Fine! What do you want to do?

SUSAN. Remember that girl who brought us that pie. I want to invite her over.

GEORGE. Oh, Janis! She's just a little bundle of sunshine!

SUSAN. Exactly. I think it'd be good for Mary to interact with someone her age.

GEORGE. That sounds like a lovely idea.

>   *(Epiphany.)*

Oh…my…god. I CAN MAKE FINGER SANDWICHES!

SUSAN. Um, sure George…if that's really what you want to do.

GEORGE. YESSSSSS!

>   *(**MARY** hears her father's triumphant exclamation and turns to him.)*

MARY. Dad, are you okay?

SUSAN. Mary, we have something to tell you.

MARY. What is it? Am I in trouble?

>   *(Excited.)*

Do I get to be grounded again?

SUSAN. Get to be?

GEORGE. No, Sparkles, we're inviting your neighbor Janis over so we can have finger sandwiches!

SUSAN. No, it's so you can make a new friend.

MARY. Oh, don't worry about me. I'm fine. I got Flopsie.

FLOPSIE. Damn right!

SUSAN. That's just it, Mary, I don't think you are. I found all of the gasoline you've been hiding under your bed.

FLOPSIE. Uh, oh. Uhhhh...I'm gonna go take a nap.

MARY. *(Aside.)* Flopsie! Don't leave me! Flopsie!

> *(The closet doors open and close. No one but* **MARY** *notices.)*

GEORGE. Gasoline! Cupcake, sure I did some questionable things in my youth, but trust me, pyromania isn't nearly as cute as you think it is. Burners never learner... burners *never* learner.

MARY. No. No. No! Listen, I've told you this before, that's what Flopsie needs to eat. Dragons need fiery stuff to grow; it's part of their diet.

SUSAN. Flopsie's a dragon?

GEORGE. I thought he was a bunny.

MARY. He's a dragon!

GEORGE. Buttercup, he could be a unicorn, griffin, or jackalope for all I care. He isn't real.

MARY. But you had Farmsworth!

GEORGE. That was a joke!

MARY & SUSAN. It was?

GEORGE. It was!

MARY. Still, I'm not a pyromaniac! Flopsie is real!

> *(***GEORGE*** is unravelling. His cheerful demeanor is beginning to crack. Slowly but surely his words will stutter and his eye will twitch until, finally, he'll explode.)*

GEORGE. Mary. Stop lying. You can't use your *fake* dragon to solve every problem.

MARY. He's not fake! He broke that chair!

GEORGE. I SAID STOP LYING! *You* broke that chair, Mary!

> *(***MARY*** starts to retreat. With every step she takes backward, ***GEORGE*** advances on her.)*

MARY. *(Frightened.)* Quit saying my name like that.

GEORGE. Don't tell me what to do you little brat!

SUSAN. George!

MARY. Dad!

GEORGE. Shut up! Both of you! You are going to start behaving properly, you are going to be very nice to Janis when she comes over, AND YOU ARE GOING TO ACCEPT THAT FLOPSIE DOESN'T EXIST!

SUSAN. GEORGE, STOP IT!

> *(As if he was in a trance, **GEORGE** immediately switches back to his jubilant self.)*

GEORGE. Okie-dokie then. I'm gonna go make me some finger sandwiches!

> *(He exits. A long pause.)*

MARY. What just happened?

SUSAN. I'm not sure.

> *(Blackout.)*

Scene Six: Flight

(**MARY** *is alone in her room with* **FLOPSIE**.
They're arguing.)

MARY. I can't believe you left me all alone like that!

FLOPSIE. What was I supposed to do?

MARY. I don't know...maybe show yourself to my parents!

FLOPSIE. That's a stupid idea.

MARY. Why?

FLOPSIE. Because you can never trust an adult. My parents told me they'd be back, and that was a lie. If I showed myself to your parents they'd be terrified. They would only see me as a monster, and then they'd take you away from me.

MARY. My parents would never do that.

FLOPSIE. Are you sure? I heard the way your dad talked to you. Actually, I wouldn't call that talking at all.

MARY. He doesn't like it when I lie.

FLOPSIE. No, he just doesn't like it when he doesn't get his way. You weren't being his perfect Little Mary Sunshine.

MARY. Shut up.

FLOPSIE. What? Don't like the truth?

MARY. Oh, you want to hear the truth? I'll tell you the truth –

(*There is a knock on* **MARY**'s *door.*)

GEORGE. (*Offstage.*) Mary, you have a visitor.

MARY. We'll finish this later. Now just sit still and don't say anything.
(*To her father.*) Come on in!

(**SUSAN** *and* **GEORGE** *enter with* **JANIS**; *she's decked out in designer clothes.* **GEORGE** *is carrying a tray of finger sandwiches and a butcher's knife.*)

SUSAN. And this is Mary's room. We'll leave you two alone to play.

GEORGE. I'll just put these scrumptious finger sandwiches on the coffee table.

> *(Dangerously spinning the knife around like a baton.)*

I also brought this handy-dandy knife in case you guys want to make them even smaller!

JANIS. Oh, thank you so much! You two are just as kind as can be!

GEORGE. *(Exiting with* **SUSAN.***)* Isn't she just precious?

SUSAN. I still don't think leaving them alone with a knife is the greatest of ideas.

GEORGE. Aw shush, honey, you're overreacting. They'll be fine!

> *(They exit.)*

JANIS. *(Pulling out her iPhone.)* Thank. God. Your father is such a freak.

MARY. He can be a little strange, but I'd hardly call him a –

JANIS. What's your name again? Madison? Marilyn?

FLOPSIE. I don't like this girl.

MARY. It's Mary.

JANIS. Whatever. I was close enough. Tell me Mary, do you guys have Wi-Fi?

MARY. No, not yet.

JANIS. Great, just great. How the hell am I supposed to keep my followers updated?

FLOPSIE. She's thirteen.

MARY. You're thirteen.

JANIS. And I have thirteen thousand followers. What's your point?

FLOPSIE. I'll say it again: I do not like this girl.

MARY. I told you to shut up.

JANIS. Excuse me?

MARY. No, not you.

JANIS. Not me? I don't see anyone else in this room, unless they're invisible or something. What? Does little Mary have an imaginary friend?

> (**MARY** *doesn't respond.*)

Oh, my god. You actually do! Wow, I thought it was sad enough when my parents told me I had to go play nice with the new girl next door, but this is unbelievable.

MARY. He's not imaginary!

JANIS. Oh, so you're not only sad, you're crazy too.

MARY. I'll prove to you he's real. Flopsie, reveal yourself.

FLOPSIE. No way.

JANIS. Flopsie? His name is Flopsie? Wow.

MARY. Flopsie, please!

FLOPSIE. Fine!

> (**FLOPSIE** *reveals himself. He is standing by the window.* **JANIS** *is awestruck. She walks closer to him.*)

JANIS. Jesus Christ!

FLOPSIE. Are you happy now?

JANIS. My followers have got to see this.

FLOPSIE. NO!

> (*As she takes out her phone and snaps a picture, strobe lights flicker. We hear a loud "whack" and the breaking of glass. The flashing stops. The window is broken and* **JANIS** *is gone. Her screams grow fainter and fainter until they are halted by a loud "thump" or "squish."* **MARY** *rushes to the window and looks down.*)

MARY. Oh, no.

FLOPSIE. It's okay. I've done this before. I'll just swallow her body and it'll decompose in my stomach.

MARY. What do you mean you've done this before?

> (**GEORGE** *and* **SUSAN** *burst in.*)

SUSAN. Did I hear screaming?

GEORGE. Are there any finger sandwiches left?

> (**SUSAN** *sees the broken window and rushes to* **MARY**'s *side. Meanwhile,* **GEORGE**'s *attention is occupied by the finger sandwiches.*)

SUSAN. Mary, what's wrong?

> (*She doesn't respond.* **SUSAN** *looks out the window.*)

Oh, my god. George, Janis is dead.

GEORGE. (*With his mouth stuffed with finger sandwiches.*) Say what now?

SUSAN. Mary, what happened here?

GEORGE. First pyromania, and now murder? Mary, you should be ashamed of yourself!

MARY. (*Panicked.*) No...no...I...it...it was –

FLOPSIE. It was me. Mary had nothing to do with it.

> (**GEORGE** *and* **SUSAN** *can see* **FLOPSIE**. *They grab* **MARY** *and hold her away from him.*)

See, Mary! I told you this would happen! Now they're going to take you away from me just because I'm a big, scary dragon.

MARY. No, it's because you just murdered a little girl!

FLOPSIE. I was trying to protect you.

MARY. You were trying to protect yourself.

SUSAN. Mary, I think it's time we all leave.

FLOPSIE. No one is going anywhere.

> (**FLOPSIE** *barricades the door, blocking the way out.* **GEORGE** *starts to sneak toward the coffee table.*)

MARY. Flopsie, let us go.

FLOPSIE. You don't understand...every time I have the courage to show myself to someone...their parents always ruin everything. I thought it would be different this time, Mary. But I guess it's not. It's just like the little girl who lived here before, and the boy before her.

And the one before him and the one before him! It's always the same ending, *over* and *over* again.

> *(By this time* **GEORGE** *has gotten the knife. While* **FLOPSIE** *is focused on* **MARY** *and* **SUSAN**, *he creeps up and plunges the knife into* **FLOPSIE**'*s back.)*

AUGHHHHHHHHHHHHHHHHH!

> *(A loud "thwack" is heard as* **FLOPSIE** *spins his tail and knocks* **GEORGE** *off his feet.* **GEORGE** *is then sent rolling down the room, grunting in agony as* **FLOPSIE** *"kicks" him.)*

Who do you think you are? You don't love her! I LOVE HER. You treat your daughter like trash and she is perfect – absolutely perfect. I love her more than you ever could! You stupid, stupid adult!

> *(**FLOPSIE** attacks.* **GEORGE** *recoils in pain.)*

MARY. STOOOOOOOOOOOOOOOOOOOOOOOOP!

> *(The room is still.)*

(In tears.) What are you doing?! That's my father! And no, he isn't perfect, but, by god, neither are you! He may be crazy, but at least he's not a murderer! I may be young, but I know enough to tell you that what you're doing is way beyond wrong! You can't fight your problems with violence or by demanding that things go exactly your way. Life doesn't work like that. And, if you were truly my friend – if you ever really cared about me in the first place – you...you'd leave.

FLOPSIE. But, Mary –

MARY. LEAVE!

> *(**MARY** is silent.* **SUSAN** *wraps her arms around her.)*

FLOPSIE. If that's really what you want.

> *(**MARY** nods. Flapping is heard. It grows distant...until* **FLOPSIE** *is finally gone.)*

MARY. Dad, are you okay?

(**MARY** *rolls him over. His side is bleeding heavily.*)

MARY. Dad!

GEORGE. Mary. I'm so sorry. This is all my fault.

SUSAN. No, George, it's –

GEORGE. Yes, it is. Mary, you're right; I'm not perfect... I'm far from it. I pushed so hard for what I thought perfection and happiness looked like, but...but that wasn't real.

MARY. Dad, please –

GEORGE. What's real is the two of you...and the love I have...there...there isn't a single word that can be said to rightfully express it. Please forgive me for everything I've done wrong.

SUSAN. Honey –

GEORGE. I did so much wrong! If...if...I could do it over again –

(*He cries out in pain.*)

Oh, god!

SUSAN. We need to get you to a hospital!

GEORGE. I'm not going to make it.

MARY. Not with that attitude! Sadness leads to madness my friend!

(**GEORGE** *laughs. His laughter turns into a coughing fit.*)

SUSAN. Help me get your father up.

(**MARY** *and* **SUSAN** *help* **GEORGE** *to his feet.*)

GEORGE. Do you think they have finger sandwiches at the hospital?

(*They lead him off, limping, as the lights slowly fade to black.*)

Scene Seven: Moving Day (Reprise)

*(The room resembles how it looked at the beginning of the play. There are moving boxes littered everywhere. The closet doors are closed. **MAX**, **JOHN**, and **CLAIRE** are admiring the room.)*

MAX. I can't believe I get this room all to myself!

CLAIRE. It's really quite beautiful, isn't it? Minus the scorch marks, that is.

JOHN. Nothing a paint job can't fix.

CLAIRE. Right you are!

MAX. I'm gonna start unpacking.

*(**MAX** goes to a box and begins to empty out its contents. **JOHN** and **CLAIRE** look out the window.)*

CLAIRE. Look at this view! Isn't it gorgeous? This is so amazing, John!

JOHN. I know! And the price only makes it that much sweeter.

CLAIRE. I do feel sorry for that widow though...moving so quickly after her husband's death. And her daughter was just adorable.

JOHN. Let's not focus on that, Darling. It's time we make our own memories in this mansion.

CLAIRE. We live in a mansion! I never dreamt it would be possible!

*(The closet doors open slowly on their own. **JOHN** and **CLAIRE** don't notice, but **MAX** does.)*

MAX. Mom... Dad...

CLAIRE. What is it, Max?

MAX. Did you guys see that?

JOHN. See what?

MAX. The closet. It just opened on its own.

CLAIRE. Oh, Sweetie, it's an old house. It was probably just the wind.

MAX. But we're inside.

CLAIRE. It was the inside wind!

JOHN. It's called a draft, Claire.

CLAIRE. It was a draft!

MAX. Are you sure?

CLAIRE. Yes, Sweetie. You have nothing to fear.

JOHN. Come on, Darling, let's give Max some space.

CLAIRE. If you insist.

> *(They begin to leave.)*

Love you, Sweetheart.

MAX. Love you too, Mom.

> *(They exit. A beat.)*

It was just a draft...just a draft. I have nothing to fear... I have nothing to –

> *(The closet doors slam shut.)*

Fear.

> *(Blackout. The curtain falls.)*

End of Play

PIGEON!

Garrett M. Ryan

PIGEON!, by Garrett M. Ryan of Troupe 3681 at Widdifield Secondary School in North Bay, Ontario, was presented in a staged reading as part of the Thespian Playworks program at the 2017 International Thespian Festival on June 23, 2017. The production was directed by Michael Daehn, with dramaturgy by Mark D. Kaufmann The stage manager was Charlotte Perez. The cast was as follows:

JOHN	Isaiah Hesford
TALKER / PIGEON	Rocco Hill
IVAN	Kaeleb Cogswell
MOTHER	Alexandra Rivers
AGNUS	Katie Lennon
GIRL 1	Emma Gasior
GIRL 2	Alessandra Bertoli
NATHAN	Soren Morici
WAITRESS	Kristina Cooper
MR. JEFFERIES	Porter Lance
MAN	Ryan O'Connor

CHARACTERS

JOHN – a social outcast

PIGEON – a presence, voiced offstage

IVAN – an older social outcast

MOTHER – John's mother

AGNUS – an old, senile lady

GIRLS 1 & 2 – girls from John's school

NATHAN – pet shop owner

WAITRESS – waitress at restaurant

TALKER – the narrator

MR. JEFFERIES – John's landlord

MAN – a man from John's past

OTHERS – voices and presences of John's subconscious

SETTING

Abstract New York City. Dark and gothic.
Extremely Hitchcock-inspired.

AUTHOR'S NOTES

The Others are dressed in black bodysuits and frequently speak in unison. Individual lines can and should be dispersed among them. Individual characters should look similar to the Others and blend back into them when not specified as their character in a specific scene. John sees people as all the same, and these people will fill his subconscious thoughts.

*(The **TALKER** stands in the dark, smoking a cigarette.)*

TALKER. Planet Earth. There's been a lot of strange stories that have happened around these parts, and a lot of interesting people that have drifted through these strange stories. We humans have a tendency to ignore the stories going on around us, eager to get on with our own adventures, missing the engrossing action happening right beside us. But sometimes you've got to stop and smell the roses. So, if you want to turn a blind eye, like the rest of this blasted place, you can keep on walking. But for the street rats, the gutter snakes, the hoodlums, and the rest of you freaks... This is the story of John, or as it's known in the dive bars, the whorehouses, and the alleyways: Pigeon!

*(Lights up. **JOHN** is placed on a bench in the center of the **OTHERS**, who form a semicircle around him. The set can change throughout, or can be mimed altogether. **JOHN** tosses bread crumbs on the ground.)*

JOHN. The birds always loved me. A boy's best friends are the birds, you know. When people grow tired of you, the birds are there.

*(The **OTHERS** pick up the bird seed in a stylistic way, acting as the pigeons in the scene.)*

You see, people have failed me long ago. When you come into this world screaming and crying, people are all you have. Your mother holds you and promises she'll love you and protect you until the end of time. I knew this was a lie when I was four years old. I was in trouble, and she was nowhere to be seen. How dare you claim you love someone and then abandon them when they need you the most...

(*Sighs.*)

I remember quite clearly the last time I talked to my mother.

(**JOHN** *moves from the bench to another spot onstage; his* **MOTHER** *appears.*)

Mother! Mother!

MOTHER. What is it, John?

JOHN. I was at the park feeding the pigeons...

MOTHER. Wow-ee. John does an activity that requires zero social interaction, what else is new?

JOHN. What is that supposed to mean?

MOTHER. You know damn well what it means, John. I'm so sick of this. When is the last time you prayed?

JOHN. I don't believe in God, Mother.

MOTHER. Well, I'm sure he lost faith in you some time ago as well...

JOHN. Have you been drinking?

MOTHER. How else am I supposed to put up with you?

JOHN. I don't need friends, Mother. I have the birds.

MOTHER. And would you stop calling me "Mother"? It creeps me out.

JOHN. I just wanted to tell you about the pigeons today...

MOTHER. Yes, yes, what about the pigeons today?

JOHN. Now, I'm not so sure if I want to tell you...

MOTHER. Well, go on. I'm sure you have other people in your life that would be dying to hear your stories, right?

JOHN. I just wanted to say that, it was so fantastic, a pigeon flew right up to me and took bread crumbs right from my palm.

MOTHER. John?

JOHN. Yes, Mother?

MOTHER. I don't care about the fucking birds. I wish God had told me what you were to become before he allowed me to bring you into this world.

> *(Scene change. **JOHN** moves away from his **MOTHER**, back to the bench.)*

JOHN. And I wish it was just my mother, but it seemed as though everyone that knew me had a distaste for me.

> *(**JOHN** moves to another spot. **GIRLS 1** and **2** stand around, talking.)*

No one really paid much attention to me when I was in high school, mainly because no one cared, but this led to me overhearing some things I wish I hadn't...

GIRL 1. Okay, okay! Truth or dare?

GIRL 2. Hmmm... Okay, I'll do truth!

GIRL 1. Boring!

> *(Laughs.)*

Okay, fine! Let me think! Okay, if it meant not getting struck by lightning, would you make out with John?

GIRL 2. That asshole from biology?

GIRL 1. That's the one!

GIRL 2. Jesus... That's a really hard one! Do I have to answer?

GIRL 1. That's the game!

GIRL 2. All right... If I get struck by lightning, do I survive?

GIRL 1. Yes, you'll be totally fine after some recovery time.

GIRL 2. All right, I'll take the lightning. Who wants to kiss John?

> *(They both laugh. **JOHN** moves away from the scene to talk.)*

JOHN. This phenomenon of people disliking me wasn't exclusive to people that knew me, I found. For example, I was in a restaurant once...

> *(Scene change to a restaurant. The **WAITRESS** and **JOHN**.)*

JOHN. Anyway, I'll just have a club sandwich.

WAITRESS. Yeah, I don't think I'm going to do that.

JOHN. What do you mean?

WAITRESS. We don't serve people like you, here.

JOHN. People like me? What is that supposed to mean?

WAITRESS. Freaks. Creeps. Sleazeballs. Why don't you do everyone here a favor and get out.

JOHN. Please... I just – I just –

WAITRESS. Now! Get out now!

*(**JOHN** runs out of the scene, in a frenzy.)*

JOHN. Everywhere I went people treated me like garbage! But the birds never did. And I avoided people as much as I could. Even the ones that seemed nice, I knew underneath they were waiting to hurt me. Take Agnus, for example. She would come to the park and sit on my bench every so often. I couldn't stand her constant chatter.

*(**JOHN** sits down on the bench and throws bird seed; again the "**PIGEONS**" pick it up. **AGNUS** sits beside **JOHN**.)*

I sit next to Agnus in the park, she smells like cinnamon rolls and rusted metal.

AGNUS. Who do you think maintains this grass? Do you think they have a specific guy for that? Do you think that's all he does?

JOHN. I don't know, Agnus.

AGNUS. What would his job title be? Grass man? Grass boy?

JOHN. I don't know. Probably neither of those.

AGNUS. Well, people always told me I wasn't any good at coming up with job titles.

JOHN. In what situation could that have possibly come up?

AGNUS. It's actually a real funny story.

JOHN. Never mind, I don't want to know.

(They sit in silence for a moment.)

AGNUS. Wow, would you look at those clouds.

JOHN. *(Disinterested.)* Would you ever...

AGNUS. Think it's going to rain?

JOHN. I have no idea.

AGNUS. Well, I sure wish it doesn't.

JOHN. Why's that? It's water from the sky. Probably one of the most harmless things weather can give us. What that is is a waste of a wish. Wish that a super volcano doesn't erupt and destroy all life on earth. I'm indifferent to rain. Rain stopped being a threat when we invented towels.

AGNUS. I'm just trying to make conversation, John.

JOHN. Well, I have had enough of it.

> *(**JOHN** separates himself from the scene.)*

She goes on like this, day after day, until one day I had enough of her.

> *(**JOHN** re-enters the scene with **AGNUS**.)*

AGNUS. John, do you ever get tired of feeding the pigeons every day?

JOHN. Why would you say that? Of course not.

AGNUS. I'm getting older every day, and I am tired of acting. I am tired of pretending.

JOHN. Pretending about what?

AGNUS. John, I know you don't come here for the birds, you come here for me. Damn our age difference. Damn what society would think. I love you. I haven't got much time left, but I want to spend it with you.

JOHN. *(Angry.)* No, Agnus. It's always been about the birds. They're my friends. They treat me better than humans like you...

AGNUS. *(Devastated.)* But you... You come here every single day... And...

JOHN. *(Furious.)* FOR THE BIRDS! I COME FOR THE BIRDS AND NOTHING ELSE! DO YOU UNDERSTAND ME?!

*(**AGNUS** runs away. **JOHN** leaves the scene.)*

JOHN. Not even the park was safe from these wretched people. And this was what set in motion the series of events that would lead me to creating...Pigeon!

OTHERS. PIGEON! PIGEON! PIGEON!

*(**JOHN** enters a new scene with **NATHAN** in his pet shop.)*

JOHN. Nathan, from the pet store, greeted me the same way every time I came in.

NATHAN. Welcome to Nathan's Pets. "Don't steal our pets." How may I help you?

JOHN. You've got to change that slogan, Nathan.

NATHAN. Why would I?

JOHN. It's weird! Who is it for? Is a pet robber going to walk in and go, "All right, I guess I'll leave"?

NATHAN. I don't know, maybe.

JOHN. All right. I need a new bag of bread crumbs, please.

NATHAN. Sure thing, John.

JOHN. Hey, Nathan, you wouldn't happen to know any good bird feeding spots, would you?

NATHAN. Honestly, I would have thought you'd have a good spot by now. How long have you been coming in here? Few years at least.

JOHN. Yes, I had a good spot, but it's been taken over by an emotionally fragile old lady. I'm looking for a new one.

NATHAN. Jeez, I don't know. Have you tried Central Park?

JOHN. You seriously think I haven't tried Central Park?!

NATHAN. I'm just trying to help. If it's such an issue, why don't you just get a bird of your own?

JOHN. A bird of my own? I barely have the will to take care of myself.

NATHAN. I can tell... When's the last time you took a shower?

JOHN. *(Ignoring his last comment.)* Then again, I wouldn't have to brave the streets as much if I had a bird of my own, living in my apartment. Would I?

NATHAN. I suppose not.

JOHN. All right, I'll do it! Show me to your finest bird friends!

>   (**JOHN** *leaves the scene to another.*)

I return to my apartment with a new friend. I decide to name him Steven. I admit I was hesitant about the idea, but for the first time in a long while, I feel truly happy. I've always wanted a roommate. Steven flaps his wings around my space.

OTHERS. Flap. Flap. Flap. *[Or flapping sounds.]*

JOHN. He even utters a few little chirps.

OTHERS. Chirp. Chirp. Chirp.

JOHN. When I look into his eyes, I feel him looking back, judgement free. This is what true friendship should feel like, and I never want it to end. But three days later, there was a knock at my door...

OTHERS. KNOCK. KNOCK. KNOCK.

JOHN. No one ever knocks at my door.

OTHERS. KNOCK. KNOCK. KNOCK.

JOHN. Unless...

MR. JEFFRIES. It's Mr. Jefferies! Open up!

JOHN. Unless it was my landlord...

>   (*A pause.*)

I slowly open the door.

>   (*The* **OTHERS** *make a creaking noise.*)

My landlord stands at the entranceway. I quickly hold Steven behind my back.

>   (**MR. JEFFERIES** *enters the scene.*)

Good evening, sir.

MR. JEFFRIES. John? I was doing some routine maintenance and heard some suspicious sounds coming from your apartment.

JOHN. What kind of sounds, sir?

MR. JEFFRIES. Well, it sounded like chirping. John, I have never had any real problems with you living here.

You stay quiet and out of my hair, which is nice. But I thought I was very clear about the rules. Pets are grounds for immediate expulsion from the building.

JOHN. Yes, sir. I do remember you saying that.

MR. JEFFRIES. So, am I right to assume that wasn't chirping I heard?

JOHN. I really don't know what you're talking about

OTHERS. Chirp. Chirp. Chirp.

MR. JEFFRIES. What was that, then?

JOHN. What was what? I have no clue what you're getting at.

OTHERS. Chirp. Chirp. Chirp.

MR. JEFFRIES. That! That noise! What is that?!

JOHN. I think fast. I can't get kicked out of this place... I'm so sorry, Steven.

> (*A terrible cracking noise is heard, made onstage by the* **OTHERS**.)

OTHERS. CRACK!

JOHN. His little body crackles in my hand. No more chirps would be heard. My landlord leaves. I hold my little friend close. He reminds me of a piece of paper, too crumpled to be smoothed out. I spend the rest of the night sobbing, and in the morning, I buy myself another little buddy. I call him Frederick.

OTHERS. Chirp! CRACK! Sorry, Frederick.

JOHN. As long as my landlord patrols my hallway, the process will repeat. It hurts me and I should just stop. But having these little guys makes me happy. However short their lives are. Hello, Jeff!

OTHERS. Chirp! CRACK! Sorry, Jeff.

JOHN. Hello, Michael!

OTHERS. Chirp! CRACK! Sorry, Michael!

JOHN. Hello, Anton!

OTHERS. Chirp! CRACK! Sorry, Anton!

JOHN. Hello, Anderson!

OTHERS. Chirp! CRACK! Sorry, Anderson!

JOHN. Twelve birds and forty-five days later.

OTHERS. Chirp! CRACK! Sorry, Steven the Second.

JOHN. This time, I do stop. I've had enough. My freezer is full of dead canaries. There's got to be a better way. I spend the night watching television. Various late-night programs. One catches my eye. Mary Shelley's *Frankenstein*, the 1931 version. It's old. It's slow. It's full of bad tropes from old movies. The things that make them classics for some reason. But it's the greatest film I've ever seen. The movie itself is fine, but I'm drawn in the entire time.

(Big sounds. Big movements.)

OTHERS. IT'S MOVING! IT'S MOVING! IT'S ALIVE! IT'S ALIVE!

JOHN. Man doesn't have anyone he's close to! Man feels discouraged with life, like he missed out! Man literally builds a friend! Sure, it doesn't turn out the greatest... some disaster ensues, but it's a film. It's fiction. You can't take any of that seriously. So, I come up with the perfect idea. The idea to beat all ideas. I decide to build myself a friend. I already have the parts in my freezer. Thank you, Steven! Thank you all of my birds! You will serve a purpose greater than yourselves! Two days later, I'm back at Nathan's.

*(**JOHN** changes scenes back to the pet store.)*

NATHAN. Welcome to Nathan's Pets. "Don't steal our pets." How are you today, John? Can I get you another bird, perhaps?

JOHN. I'm lovely, thank you for asking. But actually, I'm looking for your finest bird glue.

NATHAN. Uh...what?

JOHN. Bird glue, best you've got!

NATHAN. Perhaps you could explain?

JOHN. Glue, for the purpose of birds

NATHAN. I'm going to need some more clarification.

JOHN. Okay, sure. As an animal lover, I want the very best for my pet. I don't want to be giving them anything unhealthy. I buy the finest bird seed. I make sure their cages are safe and spacious. I would never clip their wings.

NATHAN. Sure, sure.

JOHN. When I crush them, I do it quickly. No pain, you know?

NATHAN. Pardon me?

JOHN. So, when I apply glue to their bodies. I want to make sure it's safe for them.

NATHAN. Oh! Well I'm sure we can find something to accommodate your needs!

(**JOHN** *changes scene back to his apartment.*)

JOHN. I arrive back at my apartment, and I now have a gallon of glue. The creation of Pigeon was...difficult. Difficult to recall, that is. It required copious amounts of glue, and since I require almost constant breathing, I inhale large amounts of "glue fumes." In a hazy, spinning memory, I recollect a voice from above. Guiding me. Giving me strength and power. Helping me create my new best friend. I haven't been religiously Jewish for quite some time, so I assume I was absentmindedly hearing some sort of late-night TV program. Luckily, the episode happened to be all about Pigeon.

(**JOHN** *faces backward during this and acts out what the* **OTHERS** *say. The* **OTHERS** *make sound effects as the narration happens.*)

OTHERS. Pigeon is a lifelong best friend, commonly made out of used or broken bird parts. In today's episode, we will discuss the process involved in the making of "Pigeon." First, the "disposer" collects the remains of at least twelve broken small birds. The disposer typically murders them coldly, in his own two hands. Next, high-strength industrial bird glue is applied to their little wings by the "sticker." Then, the "placer" mashes together random parts of the birds, deforming them grotesquely, and shaping them into a new creature altogether.

> *(The sound of thunder is made by the* **OTHERS**.*)*

JOHN. PIGEON! PIGEON! PIGEON!

OTHERS. Fun fact: "The disposer," "the sticker," and "the placer" all typically display several signs of antisocial personality disorder.

JOHN. And then...there he was! My best friend!

> *(***JOHN** *whips around. He is holding a disgusting bundle of dead birds, glued together, forcibly shaped into another bird. He sits down and holds his new friend close.)*

Pigeon and I stay up all night. I talk, he listens.

(To **PIGEON**.*)* People used to say I didn't know how to tell good stories. They would say –

OTHERS. John, you forget everyone else's side. There needs to be some objectivity.

JOHN. I know who I am. I don't need to know who they are.

(Pause. To the audience.) In the morning, I realize that Doctor Frankenstein could say something that I couldn't about Pigeon.

> *(The sound of thunder is made by the* **OTHERS** *once again.)*

OTHERS. It's alive! It's alive!

JOHN. At this point, Pigeon is nothing more than a pipe dream covered in rotting bird flesh and crusty feathers. Pigeon is and was fundamentally flawed since the beginning. A dozen or so tiny brains powering such a large vessel? Ridiculous! What Pigeon has always needed was...

OTHERS. Fun fact: John displays several signs of antisocial personality disorder.

JOHN. A warm, fresh, human brain... And I knew where to get one.

> (**JOHN** *switches scenes to Agnus's apartment. He's holding a bag.*)

It takes me a little while to find out where she lives, giving that I didn't know her last name. Even while I'm standing here, knocking on the solid oak door, I wonder how to bring up my proposition. Maybe if I find out she's an organ donor, that's good enough, she doesn't need to know what she's donating to. It's for a good cause after all. The door opens slowly.

AGNUS. John...? John, what are you doing here?

JOHN. Hi, Agnus. It's me, John...from the park.

AGNUS. Yes, I just said that – What are you doing here?

JOHN. *(To audience.)* I need to think quickly and efficiently *(To* **AGNUS.***)* I'm in love with you, Agnus. You were right, what you said to me, it was never about the birds. It's me and you against the world, Agnus. Let's start our life together.

AGNUS. John... Do you really mean it?

JOHN. *(To audience.)* Of course not.

> *(To* **AGNUS.***)* Yes, darling. One hundred times yes!

> *(To audience.)* I acted how they did in the movies. Almost sarcastically. Apparently she was too stupid to notice.

AGNUS. Oh, I love you too, John! Me and you against the world! Let's do it!

> *(The two move to the bench onstage acting as a couch.)*

JOHN. *(To audience.)* After some...well...things I would rather forget about, I knew I had to get moving fast. We were sitting on the couch, and she was yammering on about an old boyfriend when she was in college.

AGNUS. He was a real charming man, oh yes, he was. We probably would have been married if he didn't turn out to be a ghost –

JOHN. *(To audience.)* I wasn't listening to her weird story. I was too busy trying to find an opening to spin the conversation to what I wanted to talk about.

AGNUS. ...And he was really spooky too. Sometimes he'd scare me half to death when –

JOHN. Agnus! I lost my wallet the other day!

AGNUS. Oh, well that's too bad now. Do you need some money?

JOHN. No, no, nothing like that. I'm just trying to make conversation.

AGNUS. By cutting me off?

JOHN. Sorry, it just popped into my head. I'm like that, you know... Quirky.

> *(Pause.)*

ANYWAY... I had to go through the hassle of getting all new pieces of identification. A driver's license and everything. The thing I hate most about getting a new one is when they ask you if you'd like to be an organ donor.

AGNUS. Well, why is that?

JOHN. *(No idea.)* Uh...it's...it's none of their business.

AGNUS. I think if it's anyone's business it's theirs. Right?

JOHN. How would you like it if I asked you?

AGNUS. I don't think I would really mind.

JOHN. Fine. Are you an organ donor?

AGNUS. Indeed I am. See, that didn't bother me in the slightest.

> *(**JOHN** speaks to the audience:)*

JOHN. It started off a little rocky, but I figured out what I wanted to know. She's an organ donor, and I'm going to make sure she donates to a noble cause: Pigeon.

> *(**JOHN** turns back to **AGNUS**.)*

I've been thinking, Agnus! I've been thinking, and I've got exciting news.

AGNUS. Oh! What sort of news, honey?

JOHN. News of an opportunity. Agnus, how would you like to be part of something bigger than yourself?

AGNUS. Well, I suppose that it depends on what that thing is. What sort of thing is it?

> *(**JOHN** pulls **PIGEON** out of his bag and shows it to **AGNUS**.)*

What the fuck! What the fuck is that thing? I–I–

> *(**AGNUS** clutches her chest and falls to the ground. **JOHN** kneels down beside her and checks her pulse.)*

JOHN. It certainly wasn't how I expected things to go. I thought she would have been thrilled by the sight of him. The prospect of creating new life. No matter. This requires less action on my behalf. This way, I didn't have to kill her.

> *(**JOHN** pulls out a knife from his pocket, faces the back, and begins miming the motion of cutting and carving into **AGNUS**'s corpse.)*

The trick is not to think about what it is you're doing.

> *(The **OTHERS** make sounds of cutting and slashing while he carves.)*

If I close my eyes, it doesn't feel any different than cutting into a steak. A really big, tough steak. This is the brain that will power Pigeon.

> *(**JOHN** turns around, holding a bloody brain in his hands. He places it and **PIGEON** into the bag, content. Before he leaves the scene, he turns to **AGNUS**'s body.)*

Agnus... You were a rather annoying individual. And not all that interesting either. Come to think of it, you're probably better off where you are now than being alive. So, you're welcome.

> *(Pause.)*

You will always be a part of Pigeon. I can't think of any better way to repay you.

(JOHN notices something offstage, through the window of Agnus's apartment building.)

Suddenly, I notice something I'd wished I had noticed earlier. In the window across from me, a man stands, terrified. Everything is silent aside from blood dripping out of the bag I was carrying.

OTHERS. Drip. Drip. Drip.

(They keep repeating this throughout the following monologue.)

JOHN. Once my eyes focus, I can see him clearer. He's a plain-looking man wearing large, horn-rimmed glasses, clutching a watering can. I can only assume he was watering his flowers before bed, when he looked out the window and saw...well...me. Suddenly I'm overtaken with a strange urge. I don't feel guilty for what I've done, and I wish that he understands that. So, I step forward, smile, and...

(JOHN bows to the MAN in the window and then walks into a new scene, in his apartment building. He sits on the ground and begins assembling the brain into PIGEON.)

It's not an easy task to do, putting Pigeon together. The constant voices in my head don't make things easier. My brain is scared. Scared of getting caught. Scared of being taken away before I finish my beloved Pigeon.

(In this scene, the OTHERS should surround JOHN and slowly close in on him. JOHN continues to work on PIGEON, but becomes more and more frantic as the scene progresses.)

OTHERS. He knows what you did, John!

JOHN. Who does? Who knows?

OTHERS. The man. He saw you. He saw everything.

JOHN. Whatever he thinks he saw, he surely doesn't understand.

OTHERS. He thinks you killed her.

JOHN. I didn't kill her...

OTHERS. He watched you cut that brain right out of her little old head.

JOHN. She was an organ donor!

OTHERS. Was she?

JOHN. Yes! And she was already dead!

OTHERS. Because you killed her?

JOHN. I DID NOT FUCKING KILL HER!

OTHERS. He must think you did.

JOHN. Well, I don't know what I'm supposed to do about that.

OTHERS. He wants to take Pigeon away from you. He wants to send you to jail so he can have Pigeon all to himself.

JOHN. What can I do then?! Tell me what I can do?!

OTHERS. He thinks you killed her.

JOHN. Yes, I kn–

OTHERS. So, you have to kill him.

JOHN. He thinks I killed her, so I have to kill him.

OTHERS. Now you're getting it, John. Do what you have to do, and you and Pigeon can live happy for the rest of your lives.

> (**JOHN** *stows* **PIGEON** *away and pulls out the knife he used to carve* **AGNUS**.)

JOHN. I'll be back, Pigeon. I just have to take care of some things.

> (**JOHN** *moves to the front of the stage and mimes climbing up a ladder.*)

I climb up the fire escape onto his balcony. I see fear in the man's eyes. Fear of me. For some reason, it feels good.

> (**JOHN** *pulls out the knife and moves toward the* **MAN**. *The* **MAN** *backs up in fear.*)

MAN. Oh, no! You're that guy from across the street! Please! I won't tell anyone anything! Don't hurt me!

*(**JOHN** almost reaches the **MAN** with the knife, but before he does, the **MAN** laughs and extends his hand.)*

I'm only kidding. The name's Ivan. What is your name?

*(**JOHN**, confused, lowers the knife but refuses to shake **IVAN**'s hand.)*

JOHN. John. Who are you?

IVAN. I'm an admirer, you see. I saw your work on the old lady, and I must say, I was very impressed. A little shaky but it gets easier. How'd you do it? Poison?

JOHN. *(Pause.)* Heart attack...

IVAN. Hmm. Convenient.

*(**JOHN** stands still, not sure what to do.)*

I'd like you to meet someone.

*(**IVAN** pulls out a grotesque clump of organs and leaves.)*

JOHN. What the hell sort of thing is that?

IVAN. This is Cactus.

OTHERS. Cactus. Cactus. Cactus.

JOHN. What the hell? What sort of thing is that?

IVAN. A work of art. A modern masterpiece, not to mention my best friend.

JOHN. Art? Best friend? He's just a mass of bloody leaves.

IVAN. *(A laugh.)* Please, Cactus is full of only the finest parts from bankers, politicians, and business moguls. I use only the finest Japanese steel for my harvests, not to mention my perfected slicing techniques.

JOHN. My God... You've lost your mind, haven't you?

IVAN. Excuse me? I invite you into my home and show you my life's work, my magnum opus, and you tell me I've lost my mind?

JOHN. What you've shown me is the work of a lonely, paranoid, maniac!

IVAN. Maniac? You think I'm a maniac?! I'll show you a maniac, John!

> (**IVAN** *climbs over the edge of the balcony, holding* **CACTUS**.)

God help them all, Cactus.

> (**IVAN** *jumps off the balcony.*)

OTHERS. Down. Down. Down. Splat.

JOHN. If I had fallen from a high place, Pigeon could fly away and save me. Cactus didn't even try.

> (**JOHN** *mimes climbing down, quick as he can.*)

I will say, that wasn't the interaction I expected. It was much easier, which makes me wonder why the universe seems to be on my side, for once.

> (**JOHN** *hops down from the fire escape and looks at* **IVAN**'s *body and the remains of* **CACTUS**.)

For some reason, the splattered remains of Ivan and Cactus fill me with dismay. But I have to keep moving.

> (**JOHN** *moves into another scene. He slams his apartment door, breathing heavy.*)

OTHERS. SLAM!

> (*He holds* **PIGEON** *in his arms.*)

JOHN. Now would be a good time for you to come alive, Pigeon. I really need you right now.

> (*The* **OTHERS** *circle* **JOHN**.)

OTHERS. God wants you to succeed, John.

JOHN. If there was a God, sure.

OTHERS. You believe he would want you to be successful?

JOHN. Of course I do. This is a noble task. Holy, even.

OTHERS. Pigeon is a holy task. Pigeon is a disciple of God.

JOHN. But I don't believe in a God. How could I? All logic is against it.

OTHERS. All logic is against Pigeon.

JOHN. Take that back! Pigeon is not only logical, but a universal absolute!

OTHERS. But John, God wants you to have a heart. He needs you to have a heart. Pigeon is his most loved child, John.

JOHN. Of course, a heart! That's what I need! That should do the trick! Well, where can I get one? If he wants me to have one so bad.

OTHERS. John doesn't believe in God.

JOHN. No... No, I don't. I can't.

OTHERS. Someone John knows believes in God.

JOHN. Are you... Are you talking about...Mother?

OTHERS. How could she say no to donating a heart for God's favorite child? How could she say no to Pigeon?

JOHN. She wouldn't...

OTHERS. For God, she would.

JOHN. And if she doesn't understand?

OTHERS & JOHN. We make her understand.

> (**JOHN** *moves into another scenes and knocks on a door. His* **MOTHER** *lets him in.*)

MOTHER. John... What are you doing here?

JOHN. I have come to talk to you about something important.

MOTHER. I'm sure... Because you're always doing such important things, right?

JOHN. I am here to talk to you about God.

MOTHER. That's something I thought I would never hear from you.

JOHN. I suppose you could say I have had a change of heart.

MOTHER. How's that?

JOHN. In a way, you could say God spoke to me.

MOTHER. How dare you. God would never speak to you.

JOHN. Well, it was indirectly of course. The voices I hear are not ones from God himself.

MOTHER. What is it that he said to you? Something about birds?

JOHN. In a way, I suppose you could say that. But Pigeon is more than a bird.

MOTHER. Pigeon?

JOHN. Pigeon.

OTHERS. Pigeon!

JOHN. Pigeon is God's child. And I am his maker.

MOTHER. What game is this, John? What are you playing here?

JOHN. You are part of this venture, Mother. You will be the heart that powers Pigeon in his holy quest. In our holy quest.

MOTHER. Let me get this straight. This is all for God?

JOHN. Yes, Mother.

MOTHER. Let me tell you what I think. I think you've finally snapped. You've lost it. All your years of being an awful, terrible person have finally become too much for you to handle and you have snapped. I always knew you would lose it one day. I frequently waited for the phone call that would tell me you shot up your school or blew up a store in a suicide bombing. That's expected of you, John. But do not fucking lie to me. You would never believe in God's word. It will never reach you.

JOHN. *(Admitting defeat.)* Fine, Mother. I stopped believing in God a long time ago. In fact, I remember the day well.

(To the audience.) It was the first day of Hanukkah. I was four years old.

> *(Flashback: The **OTHERS** sit down as a group of children, singing songs* and playing. **JOHN** sits happily, singing a song.)*

WELL, I HAVE A LITTLE DREIDEL.
I MADE IT OUT OF CLAY.

---

*A license to produce *Pigeon!* does not include a performance license for any third-party or copyrighted music. Licensees should create an original composition or use music in the public domain. For further information, please see Music Use Note on page 3.

AND WHEN IT'S DRY AND READY.
THEN DREIDEL I SHALL PLAY.
OH, DREIDEL, DREIDEL, DREIDEL.
I MADE IT OUT OF CLAY.
AND WHEN IT'S DRY AND READY.
THEN DREIDEL I WILL PLAY.

(A **MAN** *approaches* **JOHN**.)

MAN. That's a really lovely song.

JOHN. Thanks, mister! I love Hanukkah!

MAN. You know, there's more to that song.

JOHN. There is?!

MAN. There is! And I have the lyrics! Would you like to sing them together?

JOHN. I sure would!

MAN. They're just out in my car. Why don't you come with me?

JOHN. *(To audience.)* Everything in me tells me not to go to the car.

(*A pause.*)

I wish I could say I didn't. I wish I could say we sang songs.

(*The scene changes back to* **JOHN** *and his* **MOTHER**.)

(Loud, accusatory.) Where were you?!
(Pause. Then, quiet.) Where were you...?

(*His* **MOTHER** *looks at him, unsure what to say.*)

You know what? Fuck that! I'm done with God.

MOTHER. What did you say?

JOHN. What has he done to help me?! To protect me?! What have you done?? What has anyone done?!

MOTHER. HE WILL SMITE YOU DOWN!

(**MOTHER** *grabs a knife and aims it at* **JOHN**.)

JOHN. I don't need God! All I need is Pigeon!

(She moves closer to **JOHN**.*)*

MOTHER. You will burn in hell!

(She lunges at him. **JOHN** *overpowers her and takes the knife.)*

JOHN. *(Crazy.)* I remember the song! It sounds different to me now! But it's beautiful!

(To an atonal version of the dreidel song:)

Pigeon, Pigeon, Pigeon, I made him out of birds. He can't fly yet, because he's not just one bird.

*(***JOHN*** plunges the knife into his* **MOTHER**, *who falls to the ground, dead.)*

Goodbye, Mother. You were quite vile. But your black heart will serve my purpose.

(He carves the heart out of her body with the knife. The **OTHERS** *make carving sounds.* **JOHN** *runs into a different scene.)*

This is it! This is what I have been waiting for!

*(***JOHN**, *with difficulty, shoves the heart into the rotting carcass of* **PIGEON**.*)*

There's nothing left to do but give Pigeon the final touches. I feel myself shaking with anticipation. There's so much riding on this moment.

*(***JOHN*** stands back and looks down at* **PIGEON**.*)*

Okay, Pigeon! You're all put together! Come on! You can come alive now! Come on Pigeon!

(Nothing. Silence.)

Pigeon! Pigeon, please! You have to work!

(Nothing. Silence.)

Pigeon! Please, Pigeon! You're all I have left in this world. You have to come alive!

*(***JOHN*** falls to the ground in tears. For a few moments,* **JOHN** *cries in silence. Then,*

manipulated by the **OTHERS**, **PIGEON** *begins to shake.* **JOHN** *sits up eagerly.*)

Pigeon? Is it really you?!

(A loud noise is heard as **PIGEON** *rises from the ground and hovers in the air.)*

OTHERS. IT'S ALIVE! IT'S ALIVE!

JOHN. I knew it! I knew it! I knew you would come! I have known my whole life you would come and save me from the world!

(A booming voice comes either from offstage or from an **OTHER**:*)*

PIGEON. SILENCE!

JOHN. Yes, Pigeon. Oh, please save me Pigeon.

PIGEON. I HAVE NOT COME TO SAVE YOU, JOHN.

JOHN. Wha– You haven't? Why not? What are you doing here then?

PIGEON. I HAVE COME TO TELL YOU THAT YOU DO NOT DESERVE TO BE SAVED.

JOHN. What do you mean?! I do! Please! We can get away from all these wretched people!

PIGEON. IF THESE PEOPLE ARE WRETCHED, WHAT DOES THAT MAKE YOU?

(Pause.)

LET'S TAKE A LOOK BACK, SHALL WE? AT SOME OF YOUR FAMOUS "EXAMPLES" OF THE INEQUITIES OF YOUR LIFE.

JOHN. We... We don't have to...

(The scene changes back to when the two **GIRLS** *were talking about* **JOHN**. **PIGEON**, *still manipulated by some* **OTHERS**, *floats next to* **JOHN**. *The same* **OTHERS** *should be used.)*

GIRL 2. If I get struck by lightning, do I survive?

GIRL 1. Yes, you'll be totally fine after some recovery time.

GIRL 2. All right, I'll take the lightning. Who wants to kiss John?

(JOHN turns to PIGEON.)

JOHN. That's what I'm talking about. Those girls were incredibly mean to me.

PIGEON. HMM. WELL, LET US REWIND TO CLASS A FEW DAYS BEFORE THAT INCIDENT.

> *(The actor playing the second GIRL mimes putting up her hand in a classroom.)*

GIRL 2. The answer is the Golgi bodies.

> *(Against his will, JOHN blurts out what he said from the past.)*

JOHN. You have got to be kidding me! Golgi bodies? Maybe you should spend less time on trying to fuck football players and dressing like a crack whore and more time paying attention.

(To PIGEON.) It was a joke! It didn't come out right! I have never been great at jokes.

PIGEON. AND WHAT ABOUT THIS EXAMPLE? A RESTAURANT, I BELIEVE.

JOHN. Okay, wait, I know where you're going with this, but...

> *(The scene moves to where JOHN was at the restaurant with the same OTHER playing the WAITRESS.)*

WAITRESS. We don't serve people like you, here.

JOHN. People like me? What is that supposed to mean?

WAITRESS. Freaks. Creeps. Sleazeballs. Why don't you do everyone here a favor and get out.

> *(PIGEON turns to JOHN.)*

PIGEON. BUT LET'S GO A FEW MINUTES BEFORE THIS.

> *(JOHN is, again, forced to say what he said in the past.)*

JOHN. Jesus Christ, am I going to have to deal with you as my server all night? I cannot trust a fat person to serve my food. I better not see you sneaking fries off the top. And pull up your shirt, I can see your tits.

(The scene disbands. **PIGEON** *is alone with* **JOHN**.*)*

I was just being honest. What is so bad about that?

PIGEON. THIS IS WHO YOU ARE, JOHN.

JOHN. I can change. I swear to you! If I change, we can be together!

PIGEON. NO, JOHN. YOU CANNOT CHANGE. I CAN SEE. THIS IS WHO YOU ARE DEEP DOWN.

JOHN. Pigeon! Pigeon, no!

PIGEON. YOUR MOTHER USED TO BE SUCH A SWEET LADY. KIND. FUN. CHARMING. SHAME YOU TURNED HER INTO A MISERABLE ALCOHOLIC.

JOHN. You don't understand! You don't understand!

PIGEON. I UNDERSTAND PERFECTLY WELL. I KNOW YOU BETTER THAN ANYONE EVER HAS. YOU CREATED ME THAT WAY, JOHN. YOU NEVER STOPPED TO CONSIDER THAT YOU WERE CAST OUT BECAUSE YOU WERE A TERRIBLE PERSON? AND I SAY THIS WITH SINCERITY, JOHN. YOU ARE A TERRIBLE PERSON. DEEP DOWN. TO THE CORE. AND YOU WILL BE ALONE. FOREVER. AND IT'S TOO LATE TO EVER STOP IT.

*(***JOHN*** *is in shambles.)*

JOHN. I was taken advantage of! That man! No one was there to protect me!

PIGEON. AND WHY WOULD THEY? LOOK AT YOU.

*(***PIGEON*** *begins to move away.)*

JOHN. Where are you going?!

PIGEON. I WILL FIND A BETTER WORLD. ONE WITHOUT YOU, JOHN. GOODBYE.

*(***PIGEON*** *leaves the stage.)*

JOHN. *(Weeping.)* It was supposed to be me and you, Pigeon! Me and you until the end! Come back! Please! Please, Pigeon! Come back! Come back to me! I don't want to be alone! I don't want to be alone! I am terrified of being alone, please! Don't leave me in this abyss! I want out! I want to be with you, Pigeon! Please! COME BACK!

> *(**JOHN** curls up on the floor and cries for a few moments. Then he slowly gets up and moves to the bench. The scene changes, presumably days later. **JOHN** is in Central Park holding bird seed.)*

Was Pigeon right? Probably. And without Pigeon, I was lost. The only place I had left was the park.

> *(**JOHN** sits at the bench.)*

At least I still have you guys. I will always have you guys. The birds always loved me. A boy's best friends are the birds, you know. When people grow tired of you, the birds are there.

> *(**JOHN** throws the bread crumbs on the ground. Similar to the beginning, the **OTHERS**, pretending to be birds, move to the front. None takes the crumbs, instead they just look at **JOHN**. Really stare at him.)*

Friends...

> *(The **BIRDS**, without taking the bread crumbs, slowly walk away. Not breaking their looks from **JOHN**. **JOHN** is crushed, and he sits alone. **JOHN** stares straight ahead, totally alone. The **TALKER** moves out onto the front of the stage, smoking a cigarette.)*

TALKER. Thus concludes the story of John. There's many more sick, tragic tales all around this little planet. You needn't look very far.

> *(He turns around, but before he leaves, says one last thing.)*

And if you require any assistance...I'll be around. Goodnight, and stay safe. There's a lot of freaks out there.

(He puts out the cigarette.)

End of Play

TALKING TO YOUR CHILD ABOUT DEATH

Bella Yaguda

TALKING TO YOUR CHILD ABOUT DEATH, by Bella Yaguda of Troupe 7903 at Mission College Preparatory Catholic High School in San Luis Obispo, California, was presented in a staged reading as part of the Thespian Playworks program at the 2017 International Thespian Festival on June 24, 2017. The production was directed by Phillip Moss, with dramaturgy by Judy GeBauer, and assistant direction by Lauryn Holliday. The stage manager was Alex Leader. The cast was as follows:

CLIPPER .... Desmond Jackson
"E" .... Rush Bogin

CHARACTERS

CLIPPER – When he speaks, it is unpleasant. Sad. Very old, and still a child.

EVE – A much younger child.

SETTING

A bus stop.

AUTHOR'S NOTE

Eve's absences are awkwardly long, time permitting.

*(Enter **CLIPPER**, dragging a dead dog on a leash. **CLIPPER** sits at the bus stop. After some time, enter **EVE**, who also sits, carrying a backpack.)*

CLIPPER. Hi... Hi.

EVE. I'm not supposed to talk to strangers.

CLIPPER. Okay.

(They wait.)

Why are you here?

EVE. This is the stop for my school bus?

CLIPPER. What school?

EVE. I'm not really supposed to...

CLIPPER. What grade are you in?

EVE. I d'wanna...

CLIPPER. Sorry.

EVE. I'm sorry.

CLIPPER. Okay.

(They wait.)

My bus was supposed to get here a long time ago.

EVE. Sorry.

CLIPPER. Is your bus late?

EVE. No. No, it's...

CLIPPER. I haven't seen a bus all day long.

EVE. It hasn't been a whole day yet.

CLIPPER. What do you mean?

EVE. It's only the morning.

CLIPPER. What time is it?

EVE. I dunno.

CLIPPER. You have a little clock?

EVE. What?

CLIPPER. For your hands.

EVE. No, I don't.

CLIPPER. What about a phone? You don't have a phone?

EVE. No.

CLIPPER. How come?

EVE. I'm little.

CLIPPER. Oh.

> *(Pause.)*

I don't have one either.

EVE. Why not?

CLIPPER. Because nobody wants to talk to me on the telephone. Everyone thinks I'm mean.

EVE. Oh.

CLIPPER. You think I'm mean?

EVE. I dun... I don't think so.

CLIPPER. Well...

> *(They wait.)*

I haven't seen a bus all day long.

EVE. You already said that.

CLIPPER. Well it's true. And no people.

EVE. Maybe school got canceled.

CLIPPER. Oh, a holiday.

EVE. Maybe.

CLIPPER. Maybe no work today.

EVE. I think school got canceled.

CLIPPER. Okay.

EVE. I... Okay.

CLIPPER. A holiday!

> *(Exit **EVE**. **CLIPPER** waits. He moves to pet the dog. Enter **EVE**.)*

EVE. My...

CLIPPER. It's you.

EVE. Did my –

CLIPPER. Your face. What's wrong with your face?

(**EVE** *has been holding back tears.*)

What happened to your face? Did you get hurt? What's wrong with your face?

EVE. No, I...

CLIPPER. I don't have a Band-Aid.

EVE. I don't need one.

CLIPPER. What's wrong with your –

EVE. Don't yell at me! I'm just – stop it.

CLIPPER. Stop what?

EVE. Stop being stupid.

CLIPPER. You think I'm mean?

EVE. I, no, I – Did my mom come here? Did a lady come here? Was she looking for me?

CLIPPER. I haven't seen a lady.

EVE. Have you been here the whole time? Are you still waiting for your bus?

CLIPPER. I haven't seen a bus all day.

EVE. Have you seen my mom?

CLIPPER. I don't know anyone like that.

EVE. Can...can you help me call her?

CLIPPER. I don't know.

EVE. I...

CLIPPER. Do you?

EVE. I know my mom's number.

CLIPPER. I don't have a phone!

(**EVE** *cries.*)

Why are you doing that?!

EVE. I want...

CLIPPER. It's ugly.

EVE. I...I want...

(*Exit* **EVE**. **CLIPPER** *waits. He pets the dog. Enter* **EVE**.)

CLIPPER. Oh, you came ba–

EVE. I'm waiting here for my mom, okay? I'm gonna wait here for my mom because this is where she will look for me.

CLIPPER. Okay.

EVE. Aren't I right? I should stay here cuz that's where she'll look for me.

CLIPPER. Stay here?

EVE. Yeah.

CLIPPER. With me?

EVE. Well...

CLIPPER. I'm gonna leave soon.

EVE. What? Why?

CLIPPER. I haven't seen a bus all day long, and I'm hungry.

EVE. But what if a stranger comes?

CLIPPER. You're not supposed to talk to strangers.

EVE. Yeah but what if one comes here and I'm alone.

CLIPPER. I haven't seen a person all day, but you.

EVE. Yeah, but I don't wanna be alone.

CLIPPER. You wanna talk to me?

EVE. Yeah.

CLIPPER. Am I a stranger?

EVE. Yeah, but you're...

CLIPPER. You don't think I'm mean?

EVE. I talked to you three times today, so now you're not a stranger.

CLIPPER. Strange.

EVE. Yeah, you won't hurt me because you're not a stranger anymore.

CLIPPER. I hurt everybody.

EVE. ...Who told you that?

CLIPPER. People. But I haven't seen one all day.

EVE. I d'wanna be alone.

CLIPPER. I can stay.

(They wait.)

EVE. What's your name?

CLIPPER. Clipper.

EVE. That's not a good name at all.

(They wait.)

Like for your toenails.

CLIPPER. No! No, like the boat.

EVE. What's a boat clipper?

CLIPPER. It's a boat for the ocean. With 400 sails, and mermaids! And, and you can go anywhere in it.

EVE. 400 sails?

CLIPPER. Mhm, I saw it in a picture.

EVE. Where was that?

CLIPPER. I don't remember him.

EVE. What?

CLIPPER. What's your name?

EVE. Eve.

CLIPPER. Eve, this is my dog.

(CLIPPER pulls the dog into her view.)

EVE. What's their...

CLIPPER. What is it?

EVE. Is it okay?

CLIPPER. Of course she is. Everything is okay.

EVE. Okay...

CLIPPER. Her name is Leslie.

EVE. Is she – why isn't she moving?

CLIPPER. She is sleeping.

EVE. I... Okay. Okay. Why'd you...name her that?

CLIPPER. I know a man named Leslie.

EVE. Oh.

CLIPPER. Yes, and he was my favorite person.

EVE. Oh.

CLIPPER. Yes, he was an astronaut.

EVE. Really?

CLIPPER. Mhm.

EVE. In space? Did he go to space? Did he go to Mars?

CLIPPER. I don't know.

EVE. How 'bout the moon?

CLIPPER. I don't know!

EVE. Didn't he ever tell you about it? Weren't you friends?

CLIPPER. Yes. Well...I don't remember.

EVE. I'd remember. I bet it's a good story. I wanna astronaut friend.

CLIPPER. He went away.

EVE. What?

CLIPPER. What?

EVE. Where'd he go? To space?

CLIPPER. I don't know.

EVE. Well, I mean did he come back? Did you see him again?

CLIPPER. I haven't seen anyone all day.

> *(They wait.)*

EVE. Is your dog...

CLIPPER. She's a good girl.

EVE. It's only, you shouldn't play with...ya know, cuz you could get sick.

CLIPPER. She can play fetch, I suppose.

EVE. I... Have you really been here all day?

CLIPPER. Yes.

EVE. Are you hungry?

CLIPPER. I don't remem– wait, no, I am.

> **(EVE** *pulls out a lunch.)*

EVE. Do you want half?

CLIPPER. Okay.

EVE. When my mom gets here, if your bus still isn't here, I bet we can give you a ride home.

CLIPPER. I don't know...

EVE. It's tuna fish.

CLIPPER. Okay.

EVE. Are you sure your dog's okay?

CLIPPER. Of course, I'm sure.

EVE. Don't yell...

CLIPPER. She's just fine.

EVE. I'm sorry! I just think –

CLIPPER. She's just like this.

EVE. Okay.

CLIPPER. She's a good girl. She's my favorite person.

EVE. I thought Leslie was your favorite person.

CLIPPER. Yes. Leslie.

EVE. Leslie the astronaut.

CLIPPER. Oh... I don't know. Yes.

EVE. Is he your friend anymore?

CLIPPER. Who?

EVE. The astronaut? You talk about him like he's gone.

CLIPPER. No!

EVE. Sorry –

CLIPPER. Not gone. No one just goes away. He's here. Right here, Leslie. Look!

(**CLIPPER** *sets the food on the dog.*)

Leslie makes dinners on Sunday for all of our friends!

EVE. Oh...that's...

CLIPPER. Yeah, he showed me the boats! The pictures. He was a librarian.

EVE. But...

CLIPPER. What?

EVE. I thought...

(*They wait.* **EVE** *cries.*)

CLIPPER. Why are you doing that?

EVE. I –

CLIPPER. My fault?

EVE. I –

CLIPPER. You think I'm mean?

EVE. I just want my mom.

CLIPPER. Oh.

> *(They wait.)*

You want my sandwich?

EVE. No.

> *(They wait.)*

My mom's gonna find me, right?

CLIPPER. I haven't seen a person –

EVE. Stop that!

CLIPPER. What?

EVE. Like everyone's left! Like everyone's disappeared!

CLIPPER. What? No! That doesn't happen!

EVE. It does, it can and it's really...it's really scary, okay? So stop talking about it. My mom is gonna find me. There's probably, probably been people. You didn't see.

CLIPPER. ...No. It can't!

EVE. What do you mean? Stop.

CLIPPER. You stop it! People can't disappear.

EVE. You're old. You know!

CLIPPER. I'm not anything, and you're a big liar!

EVE. Don't you know?

CLIPPER. I don't remember.

> *(They wait.)*

EVE. It can happen.

CLIPPER. How?

EVE. It's dying.

CLIPPER. Shut up!

EVE. Then stop talking like everyone is gone! Just cuz you don't believe it!

CLIPPER. Are you scared of me?

EVE. No! But I'm scared.

CLIPPER. Why?

EVE. Where is everybody?

CLIPPER. I haven't seen a person all day.

(**EVE** *throws her bag at* **CLIPPER**.)

EVE. Where is everyone?

CLIPPER. You hurt me!

EVE. Where is everyone if they're not dead?

CLIPPER. You hurt me!

EVE. My mom's not dead, she's gonna be here!

CLIPPER. Stop saying that!

EVE. If that's it…what if everyone is dead.

CLIPPER. That isn't…

EVE. Yes, it is.

CLIPPER. But why would people exist if they just go away at the end?

EVE. I don't know!

CLIPPER. But then why do we have –

EVE. Stop it! Everyone is fine!

CLIPPER. Of course, because.

EVE. My mom should be here.

(*They wait.*)

Why isn't she here?

CLIPPER. She isn't *gone*.

EVE. She must be. Why did she leave if she isn't?

CLIPPER. That's not –

EVE. It must be! She wouldn't just – Something bad must have happened!

CLIPPER. Shut up! People don't do that! Not when they love you!

EVE. I –

CLIPPER. No one can love you and be with you and take care of you and then just go away.

EVE. I want –

CLIPPER. That doesn't make any sense at all!

EVE. Where is my mama!

CLIPPER. She must not love you then!

   (They wait. **EVE** *cries.)*

 Stop.

EVE. Why do you say stuff like that?

CLIPPER. Stop that noise.

EVE. My mom loves me!

CLIPPER. Stop!

EVE. My mama loves me and she tells me every day and it's to the moon and back and she tells me every day!

CLIPPER. Be quiet!

EVE. You can't say those things! It's mean.

CLIPPER. You think I'm mean?

EVE. Yes! You're mean. And probably no one loves *you* either! Cuz no one loves mean people!

CLIPPER. Leslie loves me!

EVE. You can't even remember. I bet he wasn't even an astronaut. I bet you made him up! Because no one loves mean people.

CLIPPER. Stop that!

EVE. And it doesn't matter if he did cuz he's dead probably and so is your dog and everyone else! And my mom, my mom, my mom is –

CLIPPER. Take it back!

   *(***CLIPPER*** shoves the backpack back at* **EVE.***)*

EVE. Stop it!

CLIPPER. You started it!

EVE. Then use...use your words.

CLIPPER. What words? What words? How?

   *(***EVE*** grabs her stuff.)*

EVE. We won't talk about it then.

(Exit **EVE.***)*

CLIPPER. What? What did you say? Leslie? What did you say? No, it's not like...

*(***CLIPPER*** pets the dog.)*

But that doesn't make sense.

*(***CLIPPER*** shakes the dog.)*

I remember. Leslie. I remember you. Wake up! The moon and back. I remember. Wake –

*(***CLIPPER*** stands to kick the dog, once.)*

Wake up. But why? But why? That doesn't make any sense.

(He calls after **EVE.***)*

Hey! Nothing...dies. Why would we live? Nothing dies.

*(***CLIPPER*** waits. He pets the dog. Enter* **EVE.** *She sits at the bus stop.)*

I'm not mean, you're mean.

EVE. Fine.

CLIPPER. Yes, because it doesn't make sense.

EVE. Fine.

CLIPPER. Nothing dies.

EVE. ...Nothing dies.

CLIPPER. Yeah cuz –

EVE. Nothing dies, okay.

CLIPPER. Okay.

EVE. ...I'm not supposed to talk to strangers.

(They wait.)

End of Play

WAYLEN

Kayla Temshiv

WAYLEN, by Kayla Temshiv of Troupe 4268 at Marcus High School in Flower Mound, Texas, was presented in a staged reading as part of the Thespian Playworks program at the 2017 International Thespian Festival on June 23, 2017. The production was directed by Carolyn Cork Greer, with dramaturgy by Nicholas C. Pappas, assistant direction by Abby Messina, and sound design by Emily Hayman. Hannah Tarr was the stage manager. The cast was as follows.

BILLY	Jack O'Donoghue
BROOKLYN	Savannah Selbach
JANIE	Julie Lopez
TIMOTHY	Nathan Gayan
JACK	Liam Smith
CARRIE MAE	Athena Kintgen
MEG	Alison Dufault
EVAN	Jon Reece

CHARACTERS

BILLY FARLEY – fifteen
BRIDGET PACE – fourteen
JANIE CALLAWAY – fourteen
TIMOTHY STELLUN – fifteen
JACK LYLE – fourteen
CARRIE MAE BISHOP – fifteen
MEG ROE – fourteen
EVAN TRUITT – thirteen

SETTING

Waylen.
A small, unremarkable town in an indeterminate southern state.
March 1934.
Most of the action takes place at a clearing in a forest, next to the
Hopkins Mine.

AUTHOR'S NOTES

This is a show about wanting more out of life. The children of Waylen
do the same things every day. They spend all of their time focusing on
games and dreams but never actually venture to do what they desire.
Amid the boredom and consistency of their daily routines, only the small
things change. After a disaster occurs, the children are forced to make a
choice: Are they really content with their lives, or do they need to make
changes?

Pacing is particularly important in this show. The children should talk
fast, often cutting each other off or talking over one another. As they
mature, their speech should slow down.

Scene One

*(Tableau: Platforms, planks, pillars, blankets, trunks, and ladders form the town of Waylen. These pieces should be arranged in a way that gives the town depth and height but should be easy to take apart. The children of Waylen are standing, sitting, leaning, or posed somehow else onstage. They face the audience, still. **CARRIE MAE** carries a book; **EVAN**, a ball. **BRIDGET** and **MEG** are holding a jump rope, and **JANIE** is preparing to jump in. **BILLY** leans against a "tree," while **JACK** and **TIMOTHY** stand close by.)*

*(**EVAN** steps forward out of the frozen tableau, glances around, and addresses the audience.)*

EVAN. Waylen. A town few know about, and even fewer are proud to call home. Waylen means land by the side of the road! I learned that in school once. Not e'erybody goes to school. You only go if you're rich, or lucky. The only thing even 'emotely interestin' about Waylen is the Hopkins Mine. That's somethin', I guess. No one leaves. I never seen anyone move or nothin', so, no one really dreams of gettin' out. There's no real use of dreaming if dreaming gets you nowhere. Things don't change much. Ever really.

> *(**BILLY** races toward **EVAN**, grabs the ball from him, and throws it to **JACK**. The tableau is broken as the children rush to life.)*

BILLY. And they really don't need to!

JACK. *(Overlapping.)* Throw it 'ere!

BRIDGET. *(Singsong.)*
DOWN IN THE VALLEY WHERE THE GREEN GRASS GROWS –

CARRIE MAE. Have any of you read this? 'Course not.

EVAN. *(Quietly.)* That's mine!

BILLY. *(To* **EVAN**.*)* Beat it!

BRIDGET & MEG. *(Singsong.)*

    THERE SAT JANIE, SWEET AS A ROSE!

JACK. Got it! Catch –

MEG. *(Singsong.)*

    ALONG CAME JOHNNY AND KISSED HER ON THE CHEEK!

TIMOTHY. Give him the ball back, Billy –

JACK. Tough!

BILLY. He can barely throw it anyway!

CARRIE MAE. Are any of you even listenin' to me?

BRIDGET & MEG. *(Singsong.)*

    HOW MANY KISSES DID SHE GET THIS WEEK! ONE... TWO...
      THREE...

JANIE. You know I don't like that one!

BILLY. Can it Janie, you know they ain't talkin' about you!

JANIE. Why do you hav'ta be such a jerk?

BILLY. 'Cause you hav'ta be such a prude!

JANIE. Billy Farley, you're lucky I ain't a snitch or I'd tell
your pa on you!

JACK. Snitches get bruises! Snitches get bruises!

CARRIE MAE. It's stitches, you idiot. Snitches get stitches, it's
not difficult!

TIMOTHY. We should all just –

> *(The children all start yelling at each other,
> stopping only when* **MEG** *trips and falls in
> mud.)*

Are you alright?

BRIDGET. Your dress!

MEG. Oh, Ma's goin' ta kill me. I can't get another dress all
muddy.

> *(***MEG*** *begins picking up her things and
> straightening her clothes. Simultaneously,*
> **BILLY** *shoves* **JACK** *and runs behind a pillar.)*

BILLY. Hey, Jack, how 'bout we play war? You be the Germans and I'll be the Hopkins boy!

> *(Both boys mime fighting an epic and bloody battle in the background of* **JANIE** *and* **MEG**'s *conversation. They make gunshot noises and run around, much to the annoyance of the girls, and the admiration of* **EVAN**.*)*

JANIE. My ma can wash your dress real fast.

MEG. We can't afford ta pay you for –

JANIE. It's alright! Pa said the foreman was gonna call him in today, we're thinkin' he might get promoted! Ma and me can wash one dress no charge.

MEG. Thank you.

TIMOTHY. It's gettin' real dark, I need to get home 'fore dinner.

JACK. *(Upset.)* We didn't even get to the grenade!

BILLY. We can do it later!

TIMOTHY. *(To* **MEG**.*)* You'll be back after?

ALL. *(Ad-lib.)* I'll be there...bring another rope... I'll be late... Yeah...

> *(**MEG** hurriedly exits, followed by **TIMOTHY**, **BRIDGET**, and **CARRIE MAE**. **JACK** tosses the ball back to **EVAN** and exits. **JANIE** goes to follow **MEG** when **BILLY** goes to trip her. She glares at him. **JANIE** and **BILLY** exit, leaving **EVAN** alone. He throws the ball in the air, catches it, and then runs off.)*

Scene Two

(**TIMOTHY** *enters, walking to the meeting place, when* **BRIDGET** *catches up with him.*)

BRIDGET. Hey! Hey, Timothy! I had a question for you.

TIMOTHY. *(Hesitant.)* What kind of question?

BRIDGET. The romantic kind.

(*Catches his expression.*)

God, no, I don't like you! No, that's gross. If anything, I'd go for someone like Billy –

TIMOTHY. Billy Farley?

BRIDGET. He's an egg, I know. Sorry if I'm plain about it –

TIMOTHY. Please be, 'cause I'm awful lost –

BRIDGET. Do you have a crush on Meg?

TIMOTHY. I'm not a little boy –

BRIDGET. So you love her?

TIMOTHY. What?

BRIDGET. You do!

(*Beat, smug.*)

I knew it!

(*At this moment,* **MEG**, *carrying a jump rope, starts to walk in.* **BRIDGET** *notices her and quickly starts talking.*)

Oh shoot! I left my jump rope back at home. I'll meet y'all back there.

(**BRIDGET** *giggles and exits, leaving* **TIMOTHY** *and* **MEG** *alone.* **TIMOTHY** *turns and sees* **MEG**, *giving a small wave.*)

MEG. Where is everyone?

TIMOTHY. Bridget ran back to get her jump rope.

MEG. I have the rope.

(*Showing the jump rope to* **TIMOTHY**.)

Hey, are we havin' dinner this Saturday?

TIMOTHY. You and me? I –

MEG. Oh, not like that! My ma said yer comin' over with your ma to eat dinner with us.

TIMOTHY. Oh, yeah, Ma mentioned dinner with you on Saturday! It'll be a big dinner party.

MEG. I hate those, I'm awful sorry you have to go.

TIMOTHY. I still would've come, you know. Even if it wasn't a big dinner party.

MEG. What?

> *(Laughing, oblivious.)*

Just you and me to dinner?

TIMOTHY. Yeah!

> *(Beat.)*

I'd've come anyway.

MEG. Why's that?

> *(Laughing stops, slowly realizing.)*

TIMOTHY. I don't know...no reason.

> (**TIMOTHY** *and* **MEG** *lean closer to each other, about to touch hands, when* **BILLY** *and* **JANIE** *enter, laughing. Upon seeing* **TIMOTHY** *and* **MEG**, **BILLY** *immediately scowls and shoves* **JANIE**. *She trips him in retaliation.*)

JANIE. Billy Farley, I swear!

BILLY. Your ma would be awful mad if she heard you swear.

JANIE. Not if it was at you.

TIMOTHY. Will you two stop it?

> (**BRIDGET**, **JACK**, **EVAN**, *and* **CARRIE MAE** *enter.*)

BRIDGET. I need to get outta that house.

MEG. *(Privately.)* They still fighting?

BRIDGET. Always. Thank god Pa spends all his time up at Hopkins, otherwise they'd never stop.

JACK. Carrie Mae, can I see that book?

CARRIE MAE. No. You wouldn't understand.

JACK. Tough. Hey Evan, you bring the ball?

> (**EVAN**, *although excited to be asked for once, almost reluctantly throws the ball to* **JACK**.)

Billy, this can be the grenade! Now, you be the Hopkins boy –

BILLY. Nah, we'll play war later, let's play keep away! I'm first capt'n, and Timothy's the other capt'n.

TIMOTHY. I don't think –

JACK. Do the girls play?

BRIDGET. Why wouldn't we?

JACK. 'Cause –

JANIE. There's no good answer.

EVAN. How do you play keep away?

BILLY. *(Slowly.)* You have the ball, you keep it away from the other team, and whichever team drops the ball first loses. It's not hard.

CARRIE MAE. I'd rather read, thank you very much.

BRIDGET. *(Mockingly.)* "I'd rather read, thank you very much."

BILLY. Then you decide what happens to the capt'n of the losing team.

CARRIE MAE. I don't care.

BILLY. I have an idea...

> *(Whispers to* **CARRIE MAE**. *She goes wide-eyed, laughs, then nods.)*

Everyone okay with whatever it is I told Carrie Mae as the punishment for losing?

> *(Beat.)*

Good. I'll pick first, so Timothy, you can get the extra person. I get Jack.

TIMOTHY. Can I have Meg on my team?

BILLY. You don't hav'ta ask, it's keep away.

TIMOTHY. *(Bold.)* Fine then, I want Meg.

BILLY. I want Bridget.

TIMOTHY. I... Janie.

BILLY. You take Evan too.

EVAN. *(Quietly.)* Yes!

> *(The children murmur, stretch, and get to their places to start the game.)*

TIMOTHY. Carrie Mae, do you want to call start?

CARRIE MAE. *(Without pause.)* Start.

> *(The game begins.* **CARRIE MAE** *resumes reading. The contrast between teams is apparent.* **BILLY** *plays aggressively.* **TIMOTHY** *is encouraging but tries too hard not to be a leader.)*

BRIDGET. Billy! I'm open!

MEG. Evan, I'm on your team! What're you doin'?

EVAN. Sorry!

> *(***JACK*** *starts goofing around and bumping into* **JANIE***, who tries her best but keeps being blocked by* **JACK***.* **BRIDGET** *confronts the game very seriously.* **EVAN** *lingers around the fringes, while* **MEG** *is the opposite: energetic and determined to win.)*

JANIE. Jack, I swear!

JACK. Tough!

BRIDGET. Have y'all *ever* played keep away?

EVAN. *(Quietly.)* No.

BILLY. Over here!

> *(Billy's team wins when* **BILLY** *shoves* **EVAN** *and knocks the ball out of his hands.* **EVAN** *is crushed, while* **BILLY** *and his team celebrate.)*

Ha! Now Timothy's gotta kiss someone!

TIMOTHY. What? No, I don't!

BILLY. That was the rule! Loser kisses someone, right, Carrie Mae?

CARRIE MAE. Mhm!

BILLY. Who can we make Timothy kiss?

BRIDGET. *(Suddenly.)* Meg. Make 'im kiss Meg.

TIMOTHY. I can't!

BRIDGET. It's just a kiss.

JANIE. Yeah, people kiss all the time.

BILLY. Like you've ever kissed someone –

JANIE. Have you?

BRIDGET. God, it's not like they're doin' it!

> *(Immediately, the kids burst into shocked conversation.)*

CARRIE MAE. Bridget Pace!

JACK. Whoa –

BILLY. What's that? "Doin' it"?

> *(The children go silent, listening.)*

BRIDGET. Billy, do you not know what doin' it is?

BILLY. No... Should I?

BRIDGET. *(Plainly.)* It's sex.

> *(The uproar of the children resumes, with a new, higher level of chaos.)*

CARRIE MAE. That is a dirty word –

BRIDGET. How do you think we all got here? You're smart enough to know it's not the stork.

JACK. Whoa.

> *(Elongated.)* Whooooooa.

BRIDGET. See? Kissin's not that big a deal, 'least no babies come from it.

TIMOTHY. Okay.

> *(Stalling.)* I'm goin' to kiss you.

MEG. Got it.

TIMOTHY. And that's okay –

MEG. Okay!

BILLY. Kiss her already!

> *(He does. The kiss is quick and nervous, but lasts slightly longer than a peck. The other*

JANIE. You could always stay with me and my folks. My pa likes you, and my ma doesn't mind you *much*. We have a spare room.

BILLY. *(A long pause; he debates accepting and declining her offer, but instead shifts back to defensiveness.)* I think you're done with your folding.

JANIE. Right.

> *(Turns to leave, pauses.)*

Bye, Billy Farley.

> *(**JANIE** turns around and exits; **BILLY** walks off the opposite way. Both almost turn, but neither look back.)*

Scene Four

> *(After school. **TIMOTHY** and **MEG** see each other.)*

TIMOTHY. Do'ya want to talk about –

MEG. Yeah – I mean we probably should...

TIMOTHY. We kissed! I don't know why everyone is crazy about it.

MEG. Exactly! It's not like we're steady or nothin'!

TIMOTHY. Right!

> *(Beat. Then, very quickly:)*

Unless you want to be steady or somethin'?

MEG. *(Fast.)* Yeah, I would like that.

TIMOTHY. *(Also fast.)* Me too. Honest. So we're steady now?

MEG. *(Still fast.)* Yes, I think so... Should we kiss again?

TIMOTHY. *(Rapidly.)* I mean if you want to –

MEG. *(Promptly.)* Yeah.

> *(They kiss. This kiss is longer than the first one and far less awkward, but definitely still awkward. During the course of the kiss, or seconds before, **BRIDGET** enters. She sees **MEG** and **TIMOTHY** kiss and almost gasps, before covering her mouth with her hand. She hides behind a pillar and eavesdrops. **MEG** pulls away, laughing, then quickly goes wide-eyed.)*

My ma can never know.

TIMOTHY. She'd kill us.

MEG. Opposite really. I think all she sees for me is marryin' a nice boy, and livin' a nice simple life.

TIMOTHY. Sounds...nice?

MEG. I don't want to just be someone's wife! Ma would have me get married today if she thought I would. *(Realizing.)* Oh no.

TIMOTHY. No, what?

(Frantic, almost to himself.) I'm sorry I shouldn'ta kissed you, that was a bad idea. We don't even need to go steady –

MEG. Not that. No, I just realized why you're coming over to dinner this weekend. I think my ma's settin' us up.

TIMOTHY. Well she's done a real good job of it. I didn't even notice –

MEG. Not right now, at dinner this weekend!

(Beat.)

I guess we just beat her to it.

(They lean in, about to kiss, when:)

BRIDGET. *(Loudly.)* Meg, you here? I left my notebook with you – OH! Here it is…in your bag… Well, I'll be goin'.

MEG. I'll come with.

(Walking to BRIDGET.)

I'll see you after dinner, Timothy.

TIMOTHY. Yeah –

BRIDGET. *(Whispered, as they leave.)* Meg, did you –

MEG. Don't say a word!

(BRIDGET and MEG exit. TIMOTHY is left alone. He celebrates, then runs off. JANIE and EVAN walk on; they are by the "stables." It's quiet. JANIE has been talking for a while.)

JANIE. …So we all think he'll be promoted, which is good 'cause we need the money something awful. We won't know for sure 'til Pa comes home for dinner. I'm real nervous though.

(A pause.)

Evan, I'm tryin' to make conversation with you and you're makin' it real hard!

EVAN. Sorry –

JANIE. You could talk, then you wouldn't need to be sorry.

EVAN. Got nothin' to talk about.

JANIE. That's not true! Everybody has somethin' to talk about. I sure know I do.

EVAN. What?

JANIE. One day, I want to leave Waylen and move to California to be a picture star.

(**EVAN** *is silent.* **JANIE** *bursts out laughing.*)

I know, it's crazy! I just want to get out of here more 'n anythin'! It's my dream. What about you? What do you want?

EVAN. I don't know, nothin' really.

JANIE. Everyone wants somethin'. Say you have one wish, what do you use it for?

EVAN. I'd...I'd want you to get to go to California and be a picture star.

(*Beat. Blushing, she tries to laugh it off.*)

JANIE. No, really!

EVAN. That's my wish. You ta get your dream.

JANIE. No, no, a wish for you!

EVAN. I'd want to be a war hero... Like the Hopkins boy.

JANIE. He jumped on a grenade, he died! Why would you ever want somethin' like that?

EVAN. (*Looking at her.*) Maybe, if I saved some people, good people? Billy and the other boys would stop messin' with me.

(*As if on cue,* **BILLY** *walks by and notices them. He is about to interrupt, but decides to listen.*)

Billy's always treatin' me like dirt. I can't stand him! He's jus' some –

BILLY. (*Interrupting.*) Some...what?

EVAN. Nothin' –

BILLY. I want to know! An idiot? A jerk?

(**BILLY** *grabs* **EVAN** *and turns as if to hit him.*)

JANIE. Billy Farley, if you hit him I will tell your pa.

> *(Silence.* **JANIE** *and* **BILLY** *lock eyes.* **BILLY** *lets go of* **EVAN** *and takes a step back.)*

BILLY. I'm sorry. I don't know what... I'm sorry.

> *(He turns around and runs off. A long pause.)*

JANIE. He certainly won't pick on you no more. And if he does, I'll stop him.

> *(Smiling.)*

You and me, Evan. We can take him.

> *(A pause, then they continue walking.)*

EVAN. Janie? I have a question. It's real weird...

JANIE. What is it?

EVAN. Is Carrie Mae's first name Carrie Mae, or is it Carrie, and her middle name is Mae?

JANIE. *(Realizing.)* I have no idea!

EVAN. Me either! It's weird. We all live so close, but nobody really *knows* anybody.

JANIE. Well...now you know me! I like walkin' with you Evan, 'specially when you talk.

> *(They leave.)*

Scene Five

(MEG and BRIDGET are walking home. They stop in front of Bridget's house. BRIDGET almost enters the house, but she stops.)

BRIDGET. They're fightin'.

MEG. Don't they love each other –

BRIDGET. Either they love each other or they don't, but they need to be plain about it and just leave each other already. Especially if Ma is doin' it with Ezekiel Jacobs –

MEG. I'm so sorry, I had no idea –

BRIDGET. No one did. They used to meet up, Ezekiel Jacobs and my ma, when Pa would work late at the mine. But now Ezekiel Jacobs is workin' at Hopkins too, so when they met up Pa caught them, and I...

MEG. You're tough, you can brave a terrible dinner with your folks.

BRIDGET. Yeah, I'm tough, I'll be okay.

MEG. Okay... Bye!

(MEG exits, and BRIDGET takes a deep breath. She rolls her eyes and walks inside.)

Scene Six

(That night, after dinner. **JANIE** *and* **CARRIE MAE** *enter quietly, with* **JACK** *and* **BILLY** *following them close behind, making loud noises and pushing each other.* **EVAN** *walks on, by himself, and stands off to the side.* **BRIDGET** *runs on and slows down once she sees everyone.* **BILLY,** *attempting to be inconspicuous, crosses to* **JANIE** *and pulls her aside.)*

BILLY. I'm real sorry about everythin' earlier. You know I wouldn't ever hit Evan –

JANIE. Leave him alone.

*(***JANIE*** walks back to* **EVAN** *and begins to try and teach him a hand-clapping game.* **BILLY** *crosses to* **JACK** *and they begin to play catch.* **MEG** *enters and stands by* **BRIDGET.** *They talk quietly while everyone else plays, or, in* **CARRIE MAE***'s case, reads.* **TIMOTHY** *enters and joins the game of catch, careful not to stand too close to* **MEG.***)*

MEG. How was dinner?

*(***BRIDGET*** shakes her head "no," and the girls are quiet.* **JACK** *catches the ball and hands it to* **EVAN,** *crossing to* **CARRIE MAE.***)*

JACK. Hey, Carrie Mae! Why d'you bring that book wherever you go? Is it even worth readin'?

CARRIE MAE. *(Barely looking up from her book.)* It's the only thing in this town that's *worth* anything.

JACK. Why?

CARRIE MAE. 'Cause it'll get me out of here.

JACK. Why's you want to leave so bad, Carrie Mae? You not like us or somethin'?

CARRIE MAE. No, no, it's not that.

(Beat, everyone notices a shift.)

CARRIE MAE. I just know there are bigger things out there than this town. If I keep readin', learnin', maybe I can go out there and...fix things.

JACK. What all needs fixin'?

CARRIE MAE. People get awful sick here sometimes –

JACK. Do you mean how the workers always cough –

BILLY. From the mine?

CARRIE MAE. The book's about modern medicine. I figure, if I read enough about it all, I can find out why all our workers are gettin' sick.

BILLY. *(Sarcastically.)* You want ta be a miracle doctor, Carrie Mae?

JANIE. At least she could get out of this town someday.

BILLY. What, do you want to leave too?

> *(A moment, everyone shifts. They all realize that, maybe, none of them actually like the way they've been living. Maybe, Waylen isn't where anyone wants to be.)*

JANIE. Would that be so bad?

> *(Beat.)*

I've always wanted to move to California. Don't you think of leavin'?

BRIDGET. I do!

BILLY. My pa is talkin' about makin' me work in the mine as soon as there's an openin' –

JANIE. Billy –

BILLY. I'll leave Waylen before I work there.

> *(Pointing at the mine, nearby.)*

People get hurt! I don't want to. I wish the Hopkins's never came to this town and built that stupid mine.

CARRIE MAE. It's a memorial for a hero! And the mine is the only thing putting food on all our tables! Without it, our families would starve.

JANIE. Like mine.

(A long pause.)

My pa doesn't work at Hopkins anymore.

MEG. You said he was getting promoted –

JANIE. We were wrong. They fired him.

EVAN. *(Quietly.)* I'm sorry. I know you –

JANIE. It's alright.

(To BILLY.) I hate the mine too.

(Another long pause. MEG tries to lighten the situation.)

MEG. What would you do, Bridget? If you got outta here?

BRIDGET. Go to the beach. After that, who cares?

MEG. I would get away from my controllin' mother.

(Laughing.)

She may drive me insane one day.

BRIDGET. Maybe you'll be as crazy as her.

MEG. Never!

TIMOTHY. I can't imagine leaving, but I can't imagine stayin' either.

(When CARRIE MAE is distracted, JACK takes her book and starts flipping through the pages.)

Waylen...me and my ma...that's all I've ever known.

MEG. But if you could – go anywhere, I mean. What would you do?

(TIMOTHY shrugs and is about to answer when CARRIE MAE catches JACK with her book and screams. Everyone jumps.)

CARRIE MAE. Give that back!

JACK. I was just –

CARRIE MAE. Give me back my book –

(CARRIE MAE tries to grab the book from him, misses a few times, then catches it. They both pull, and the book tears in half. MEG grabs TIMOTHY's hand. CARRIE MAE stands very still.)

JACK. I'm so sorry.

CARRIE MAE. I hate you.

JACK. Carrie Mae –

CARRIE MAE. I hate you!

> *(She storms away on the verge of tears, clutching the broken book.* **JACK** *runs after her.)*

BILLY. What is he doing?

> *(***BILLY** *sneaks closer to them and listens.)*

JACK. I'm sorry 'bout your book!

CARRIE MAE. Why did you take it anyway?

JACK. You never put it down, I thought – I don't know. It's stupid, because I can't even – it's stupid.

CARRIE MAE. *(Turning.)* You can't what?

JACK. I said it's stupid –

CARRIE MAE. Can't even what?

JACK. Read! I can't read, okay? I thought, maybe, I could figure out your book and be smart like you.

CARRIE MAE. I didn't know. I'm –

> *(She notices* **BILLY** *and stops.)*

I'm goin' home.

> *(She runs off.* **JACK** *glares at* **BILLY**, *then runs after her.* **BILLY** *rejoins the group.)*

BRIDGET. *(To* **MEG** *and* **TIMOTHY**.*)* Anyone goin' to mention you two've been holding hands this entire time? No? Well, I think it's cute.

MEG. What? I –

BRIDGET. Go, run along, be cute!

> *(Laughing,* **MEG** *and* **TIMOTHY** *walk off.* **BILLY** *and* **BRIDGET** *leave as well.* **JANIE** *looks at* **EVAN**.*)*

JANIE. What about you?

EVAN. ...What about me?

JANIE. Don't you want to leave Waylen?

EVAN. I don't know. Nobody's ever thought to ask.

JANIE. Well, I'm asking.

EVAN. I don't think 'bout it much...

JANIE. Just 'cause you're quiet doesn't mean you're not thinkin'.

>   *(Beat.)*

You don't actually hav'ta leave... It's just a dream.

EVAN. I've never had one.

JANIE. You should try it sometime!

>   *(Laughing.)*

G'night, Evan.

EVAN. G'night. Janie?

>   *(Beat.)*

I think I would like to leave Waylen.

>   *(**JANIE** smiles, then exits, leaving **EVAN** alone. A long pause.)*

I could have a dream.

>   *(He goes to continue, when a quiet rumbling is heard. It grows until it is apparent something is wrong. **JANIE** runs back on. As the children yell, sounds of glass shattering and buildings collapsing are heard. Throughout the rest of this sequence, the children tear down the pillars, ladders, and trunks and rearrange the town of Waylen.)*

JANIE. What was that?

EVAN. I –

>   *(**BRIDGET** runs on. **TIMOTHY** and **MEG** follow.)*

TIMOTHY. Do you hear that –

BRIDGET. Anyone feel it shaking?

>   *(**BILLY** runs on and crosses to **JANIE**.)*

BILLY. The hell is this?

JANIE. I don't know!

MEG. This isn't okay. Somethin's wrong.

(*A scream offstage.* **JANIE** *heads toward it.* **BILLY** *grabs her arm.*)

JANIE. What was –

BILLY. Stop it!

MEG. That was Carrie Mae!

(**MEG** *runs toward the scream but is stopped by* **JACK** *and* **CARRIE MAE** *entering.*)

CARRIE MAE. It's an earthquake!

BRIDGET. What do we do?

CARRIE MAE. I–I–I'm not sure! Hide in doorways –

BILLY. We're outside! There are no doorways!

TIMOTHY. It's going to be okay, honest!

MEG. (*Shocked, realizing.*) It's not an earthquake. Look!

(*Pointing out.*)

It's the mine.

BRIDGET. Oh my god!

(*Sobbing.*)

My pa's in there!

CARRIE MAE. We're too close!

TIMOTHY. It's going to be okay –

(*As they speak, set pieces are tipped over, the rumbling grows louder, and crashes are heard.*)

MEG. It's not goin' to be okay!

(**TIMOTHY** *tries to hold onto* **MEG**, *but she pushes him off and runs away.* **JACK** *pushes* **CARRIE MAE** *toward the large group, then runs to bring back* **MEG**. *Everyone's screams overlap as the rumbling reaches a peak and* *the mine explodes.* **JANIE** *tries to follow them, but* **BILLY** *grabs her and holds her back.)*

JACK. I'll be right there!

CARRIE MAE. Jack –

TIMOTHY. Meg!

BILLY. Janie, stay here!

BRIDGET. Everything's fallin' apart –

TIMOTHY. Meg, be careful!

(**JANIE** *shoves off* **BILLY** *and runs after* **MEG**, *but she is stopped by* **EVAN**.)

JANIE. Evan, what're you –

(*A pillar starts to tip over on top of* **JANIE**, *but* **EVAN** *pushes her out of the way and it falls on him.)*

Evan!

BILLY. Janie, watch out!

MEG. I can't breathe!

BRIDGET. Come here!

TIMOTHY. Meg!

(*The group scatters. The children fall down amid the wreckage. It goes quiet. A long pause. Slowly,* **JANIE** *starts to move. She coughs a few times and looks around.)*

JANIE. Is everyone okay?

(*No reply. The town is still.)*

Please be okay.

(*Silence.)*

Is anyone –

BILLY. Yeah! Yeah, I'm okay!

JANIE. Oh, thank god!

BRIDGET. Me too!

JANIE. Everyone else must be –

CARRIE MAE. Help! I'm stuck!

> (**BILLY** *and* **JANIE** *rush to help* **CARRIE MAE** *and quickly get her out from under a ladder.* **BRIDGET** *slowly gets up and joins them.*)

Thank you.

TIMOTHY. *(Waking up.)* Where's Meg?

BILLY. *(Beat.)* I don't know.

> (**TIMOTHY** *jumps up and the five children start searching through the wreckage.* **BILLY** *looks out and stops cold, staring.*)

BILLY. Janie...

JANIE. Yeah?

BILLY. The mine...it's gone.

> *(The children go silent, shocked. Slowly,* **MEG**, **EVAN**, *and* **JACK** *come to the front.)*

EVAN. So...this is what it feels like to leave Waylen.

> *(Lights fade out.)*

Scene Seven

*(A week later. The town is still in ruins. It is about the time that the children of Waylen would be returning from school or work. The ball and jump rope lie discarded in the wreckage. It is really, truly quiet. Throughout the rest of the show, **EVAN** should sit off to the side and observe. All the living children should cough periodically, as if not all of the smoke has settled. **CARRIE MAE** and **BILLY** are sitting. **CARRIE MAE** reads. **EVAN** looks at them for a minute, then looks away. **JANIE** walks on and crosses to **CARRIE MAE**. **EVAN** sits up.)*

JANIE. I didn't think anyone would come. I know Timothy doesn't want to, and Bridget – she's with her ma today. If you two want to come over to my place for dinner tonight, you're welcome to.

(A pause.)

Carrie Mae, you fixed your book!

(Beat.)

I'm goin' ta go help set up. Lots of food ta make.

*(**JANIE** exits. There is a long pause.)*

CARRIE MAE. I told him I hated him, and then he died. Jack's dead and the last thing I said was I hate him.

*(**CARRIE MAE** exits. **BILLY** leaves in the other direction.)*

Scene Eight

(Timothy's house. **BRIDGET** *runs on and knocks on the door.)*

BRIDGET. Timothy? Timothy, you home?

(Silence.)

I'm comin' in, okay?

(She walks in and finds **TIMOTHY** *sitting on the floor.)*

Hi.

TIMOTHY. I'm sorry about your –

BRIDGET. Why does everyone say that? Doesn't mean anythin'.

(Beat.)

I just came to say...if you need anyone, I'm here. If you don't...good. I'm really sick of talking about everythin'.

TIMOTHY. Me too, honest.

(After a pause.) It's so quiet now. I hate livin' alone.

BRIDGET. Nobody visit you, or bring you food?

(Beat.)

Have you eaten anything today?

*(**TIMOTHY** shakes his head "no.")*

Yesterday?

*(**TIMOTHY** shakes his head "no" again.)*

Have you not eaten at all this last week?

(No reply.)

Timothy, what are you doin'?

TIMOTHY. *(Tense.)* I want to be alone.

BRIDGET. We all lost Meg. I know what you're –

TIMOTHY. No you don't. Meg was my... You wouldn't understand.

BRIDGET. She was my best friend –

TIMOTHY. I lost her! I lost my ma!

BRIDGET. I lost my pa, doesn't that count?

TIMOTHY. You still have one parent left –

BRIDGET. *(Exclaims.)* It's not a contest! And if it was... I sure don't want to be winnin'. God...Timothy. I thought, maybe, someone else knew what I was goin' through and we could figure it out together. But no.
(Hurt.) I forgot...you have it *so* much worse.

    (Beat.)

I'm sorry your ma got sick, I'm sorry she died, and I'm sorry you won't let me try to help you.

    (She scoffs.)

Goodbye, Timothy.

    *(**BRIDGET** leaves. A pause. **TIMOTHY** reaches into one of the trunks and pulls out a gun. He turns it over a few times in his hands, then places it on the floor in front of him.)*

Scene Nine

(By the wreckage. **EVAN** *is still sitting off to the side.* **JANIE** *is walking home carrying a basket of assorted fruits and vegetables.* **CARRIE MAE** *walks past with her nose in her book.)*

JANIE. Carrie Mae?

CARRIE MAE. I'm reading.

JANIE. Your book's upside down.

*(***CARRIE MAE*** *realizes and flips the book so it is the correct way. Tears are in her eyes.)*

Carrie M–

CARRIE MAE. *(Cold.)* Just leave me alone.

JANIE. What is wrong with you?

CARRIE MAE. *(Beat.)* I don't know. I don't know –

(She sits on the ground, crying. **JANIE** *puts her basket down and sits with her.)*

I don't even know why I'm crying, I just can't stop!

(Crying, she starts laughing.)

I hate not knowing things.

(They both laugh. Tentatively, **JANIE** *tries to comfort* **CARRIE MAE**.*)*

Everythin's a mess here now. It's been a week and nobody's even tried to fix up this town. All they care about is rebuildin' the mine.

JANIE. *(An idea.)* You should do it. Work on fixin' the town until you can make us live forever or somethin'!

CARRIE MAE. *(A moment of excitement.)* I'd like that.

(Laughing, **JANIE** *stands.* **BRIDGET** *walks on, sees them, and stops.)*

JANIE. Good. I have to go get home for the dinner tonight. Pa's out late rebuildin' the mine, as he's the new assistant manager and all –

BRIDGET. Your pa, he's the new assistant manager?

JANIE. They hired him back –

BRIDGET. That's my pa's job. They've already replaced him?

JANIE. I'm sorry –

BRIDGET. Shut up, oh my god, just shut up.

    (Rushed.) I need to go.

> (**BRIDGET** *runs off.* **JANIE**, *nearing tears, tries to shrug at* **CARRIE MAE**, *then decides to leave as well.* **EVAN** *watches her go. Eventually,* **CARRIE MAE** *exits, leaving* **EVAN** *alone.)*

Scene Ten

*(Timothy's house. **TIMOTHY** is on the floor, shaking. He's attempting to load the gun, but he keeps dropping different pieces. He figures it out and lifts the gun to his head. As he reaches for the trigger, **BRIDGET** enters with a plate of food. She drops it and screams.)*

BRIDGET. What are you doin' –

TIMOTHY. Bridget –

BRIDGET. What's happened to you?

TIMOTHY. I don't have anything here –

BRIDGET. You're a bigger idiot then Billy Farley and that's sayin' somethin' –

TIMOTHY. I just want to...stop.

BRIDGET. Well, that's not gonna happen, I won't let you –

TIMOTHY. You pity me, 'cause of Meg –

BRIDGET. I don't pity you, and this isn't because of Meg.

*(Beat. **BRIDGET** changes her tactics.)*

I get it: the world is awful. I'm not goin' to tell you to chin up and put one foot in front of the other, 'cause tomorrow will be better. I don't know. Tomorrow could be even worse, but you can't just quit when things get difficult. You've got to fight. I want to help you, Timothy. Let me.

*(Very slowly, **BRIDGET** picks up the gun. Silence. She attempts to move it away from **TIMOTHY**, when he notices.)*

TIMOTHY. No –

*(**TIMOTHY** lunges for the gun and **BRIDGET** pulls it away, raising it above her head. They fight, breathing heavily, until **TIMOTHY** grabs her wrist and pulls **BRIDGET** close to him. For a moment, their eyes lock. Desperately, **TIMOTHY** pulls **BRIDGET** in and kisses her.*

She drops the gun and kisses him back, and **TIMOTHY** *takes off* **BRIDGET**'s *cardigan. She starts to pull off his shirt when he stops.)*

Wait.

(A pause. He stares at her for a few seconds, then continues kissing her. The lights fade out, leaving them in darkness.)

Scene Eleven

(Outside the Callaway house. **BILLY** *runs up and loudly knocks on the door. After a second, he knocks again, louder.)*

JANIE. One minute!

*(***JANIE*** *walks over to the door and opens it, seeing* **BILLY**. *He grabs her arm, pulls her outside, and closes the door.)*

What are you doin'?

BILLY. You said if things were bad I could always stay with you –

JANIE. You can.

(Beat.)

Now might not be a good time though.

*(***BILLY*** *starts to leave.)*

Wait.

(Beat.)

Do you want ta go out for a walk? We can talk 'bout it.

BILLY. You sure?

JANIE. They won't even notice I'm gone.

BILLY. Okay...okay.

*(***BILLY*** *and* **JANIE** *walk out into the clearing where* **EVAN** *has been sitting. He watches them intently.)*

My dad says he thinks the mine explodin' is my fault. That I "wronged God" too many times, so he took it out on the town. He says all my troublemakin' caught up with me.

JANIE. Well, my ma is currently hosting a dinner party when we all know we oughta be havin' a funeral.

BILLY. I wished there wasn't a mine, and now it's gone.

JANIE. You do know it's not your fault –

BILLY. My pa wants me to start workin' there once it's rebuilt, since there's so many job openin's now.

JANIE. I'm sorry.

>   *(Beat.)*

BILLY. I miss Jack.

JANIE. I miss Evan.

>   *(**EVAN** sits up.)*

BILLY. Evan?

JANIE. Evan. I know you two hated each other –

BILLY. I didn't –

JANIE. You sure acted like it.

>   *(Beat.)*

He died savin' me, you know that? I never did anythin' worth savin' me for.

BILLY. *(Quietly.)* You're worth protecting.

JANIE. I hate this town! It's like the only way you can actually leave is –

BILLY. Dyin'?

JANIE. Dyin'.

>   *(Beat.)*

BILLY. Why?

>   *(Beat.)*

Why don't we just leave right now? What's here for us? A life workin' in the mine, breathing air that'll kill us? I don't want that, and I know you don't. Why don't we just run away? We can even go to California if you want! Come with me. Just leave and never look back. Never.

>   *(Beat. **JANIE** realizes.)*

JANIE. Okay.

>   *(Beat.)*

If you want ta up and leave, I will too.

BILLY. You're serious? We can leave tonight if you want. I can take my pa's car –

JANIE. And I can pack my things durin' the dinner party. We can meet up back here and just leave!

> *(Laughing, they hug. They pull away, then* **BILLY** *leans in closer to* **JANIE** *and she shoves him.)*

(Exclaims.) Billy Farley! Were you 'bout to kiss me?

BILLY. *(Covering.)* No? I was jus–

JANIE. Don't even think about it! Just 'cause we're runnin' away together doesn't change the way I think about you.

BILLY. Well, I still think you're –

JANIE. A prude?

BILLY. No!

> *(Beat.)*

Stubborn.

JANIE. Good.

> *(***BILLY*** goes to leave.)*

Billy?

> *(Beat, he stops.)*

Are we crazy?

BILLY. We're gettin' out of Waylen, who cares?

> *(He exits.* **JANIE** *stands up, laughs, and starts to walk off, when* **EVAN** *stands up.* **JANIE** *stops. She reaches into the rubble and pulls out the ball. She tosses it once in the air.* **EVAN** *crosses so he is standing right in front of her. He tries to reach her, to hold her there, but he can't.* **JANIE** *tosses the ball in the air once, then places it on the ground. She sighs, turns, and ends up inches away from* **EVAN***. For a moment, it is like she can see him.* **EVAN** *grows hopeful, but the moment passes and*

JANIE *walks away.* EVAN *picks up the ball. He looks out at the audience, then puts the ball back down.)*

Scene Twelve

(Timothy's house, later that night. BRIDGET is putting clothes back on. TIMOTHY stands by her.)

BRIDGET. We're both upset, we're grievin'. That wasn't supposed to happen –

TIMOTHY. It didn't feel...wrong.

BRIDGET. It was! Not...what we did, but that it was us. It was always you and Meg. It should have been.

(Shift.)

What do we do now?

TIMOTHY. I don't know.

BRIDGET. Grow up, I guess.

TIMOTHY. I don't know how. My pa didn't stick around long enough to teach me.

BRIDGET. Well, my ma isn't exactly a great role model.

TIMOTHY. I guess we're gonna have to figure things out ourselves.

BRIDGET. No, we can figure it out together.

(A shift, realizing.)

We're not kids anymore, are we?

TIMOTHY. I don't think so.

*(**TIMOTHY** picks up the gun they left on the floor and puts it in a trunk. He crosses to **BRIDGET**, takes her hand, and they walk into another room.)*

Scene Thirteen

(The forest, during the dinner party. **EVAN** *sits alone.* **JANIE** *enters, carrying a pillowcase stuffed with her belongings, and runs into* **CARRIE MAE**.*)*

CARRIE MAE. Janie! I'm on my way to your party! Why aren't you there?

JANIE. *(Beat, she decides.)* Can you keep a secret?

CARRIE MAE. That depends...what is it?

JANIE. I'm leavin', tonight. Me and Billy are meetin' –

CARRIE MAE. You're runnin' away with Billy Farley?

JANIE. *Please* don't tell anyone! Just for tonight! Then we're gone.

CARRIE MAE. Okay, okay! I won't tell.

JANIE. Thank you!

(She starts to run off and then stops.)

Carrie Mae?

(Beat.)

Your first name, is it Carrie Mae? Or is it Carrie, and your middle name's Mae?

*(***EVAN*** smiles.)*

CARRIE MAE. It's Carrie Mae. My middle name's Edith, if that helps any. Why?

JANIE. *(Shrugging.)* No reason.

(She starts to exit.)

CARRIE MAE. Good luck.

*(***CARRIE MAE*** goes into Janie's house as* **BILLY** *walks on, carrying a backpack.)*

BILLY. I have the car parked down the street, you ready?

*(***JANIE*** nods. Smiling,* **JANIE** *and* **BILLY** *run off.)*

Scene Fourteen

(The next morning. The town of Waylen is finally calm. This is the wonderful stillness after a tragedy has subsided. The three children of Waylen, and **EVAN**, *are in the clearing.)*

BRIDGET. Billy and Janie gone and ran away together!

CARRIE MAE. *(Feigned surprise.)* Really? Janie, run away with...him? Wow. I had no idea.

TIMOTHY. I heard it too. Well, I heard it from Bridget.

(They all laugh.)

BRIDGET. They actually made it out.

TIMOTHY. Imagine what Meg and Evan and Jack would have said.

BRIDGET. Meg would have cackled!

CARRIE MAE. "Tough," Jack would have said, "Tough."

TIMOTHY. Evan – I don't know, Evan didn't really say much.

(A moment.)

BRIDGET. Hey Timothy, want to jump rope? I can teach you. It's pretty easy. Carrie Mae can help too.

TIMOTHY. Alright

*(**BRIDGET** grabs the jump rope from the wreckage and begins jumping rope with **CARRIE MAE** and **TIMOTHY**. Immediately, something is off.)*

BRIDGET. Down in the valley where the green grass grows...

(She trails off and puts down the jump rope.)

I think we've outgrown that.

(The three former children look around the clearing.)

TIMOTHY. I guess Waylen won't be quite what it used to be.

BRIDGET. Maybe that's okay.

TIMOTHY. Maybe it is.

> (**EVAN** *takes a few steps forward and looks out.*)

EVAN. That's 'bout it. For a little while, just 'bout a week, things really, truly, changed 'round here. People left...

> (*It is as if fifteen years have passed.* **JANIE** *and* **BILLY** *enter. As they speak, they become adults.*)

JANIE. I made it to California –

BILLY. We made it to California. It was hard at first, but we figured it out. I was drafted, and I ended up working as a mechanic for a while before I saw action.

JANIE. I missed him, and I worried. Which was stupid, 'cause nothin' could ever kill Billy Farley.

BILLY. When I made it back, I learned to fix cars and got a steady payin' job. I never worked in a mine, and I didn't become like my pa.

JANIE. I didn't become a big picture star, but I got to have my own life.

BILLY. We still argue, often, but –

JANIE. We're very happy.

EVAN. And people stayed.

> (**CARRIE MAE, TIMOTHY,** *and* **BRIDGET** *enter, now adults.*)

CARRIE MAE. I never left Waylen. Not once. But I helped rebuild the town, finished school, and now I teach the children of Waylen to read. I'm not married, I'm not very social, but I have an awful lot of books and I'm makin' a difference. I am.

> (**TIMOTHY** *and* **BRIDGET** *hold hands and laugh.*)

TIMOTHY. We grew up.

BRIDGET. And got married.

TIMOTHY. I fought in the war, but I made it back to my family safely. I work in the mine.

BRIDGET. I watch our kids. We live the traditional Waylen life.

TIMOTHY. Things aren't always easy.

BRIDGET. But we're here for each other, every time things get difficult.

EVAN. And me? And Jack and Meg? We couldn't stay here forever, even if we wanted to.

>*(**MEG** and **JACK** enter, look at **EVAN**, smile, and everyone returns to their opening poses. Only **EVAN** remains center.)*

The land by the side of the road.

>*(Beat.)*

That just 'bout sums it up. Livin' simple, borin' lives. Wishin', instead of doin'.

>*(Beat, a shift.)*

Maybe you spend all your time dreamin' of gettin' out, maybe you don't... That makes the difference though. Wantin' to leave. That makes all the difference.

>*(**EVAN** looks around.)*

So...that's Waylen.

>*(He places the ball on the ground, takes one last look out into the audience, then joins the others in their tableau.)*

Maybe things do change.

>*(He looks around at the others and then back at the audience. He smiles. Lights fade to blackout.)*

End of Play